AMAZING STORIES

Edited By Sarah Olivo

First published in Great Britain in 2020 by:

 Young**Writers**® — Est. 1991 —

Young Writers
Remus House
Coltsfoot Drive
Peterborough
PE2 9BF
Telephone: 01733 890066
Website: www.youngwriters.co.uk

Printed and bound in the UK by BookPrintingUK
Website: www.bookprintinguk.com
YB0437I

FOREWORD

Welcome, Reader!

Are you ready to enter the Adventure Zone? Then come right this way - your portal to endless new worlds awaits. It's very simple, all you have to do is turn the page and you'll be transported into a wealth of super stories.

Is it magic? Is it a trick? No! It's all down to the skill and imagination of primary school pupils from around the country. We gave them the task of writing a story on any topic, and to do it in just 100 words! I think you'll agree they've achieved that brilliantly – this book is jam-packed with exciting and thrilling tales.

These young authors have brought their ideas to life using only their words. This is the power of creativity and it gives us life too! Here at Young Writers we want to pass our love of the written word onto the next generation and what better way to do that than to celebrate their writing by publishing it in a book!

It sets their work free from homework books and notepads and puts it where it deserves to be – out in the world and preserved forever. Each awesome author in this book should be **super proud** of themselves, and now they've got proof of their ideas and their creativity in black and white, to look back on in years to come!

We hope you enjoy this book as much as we have. Now it's time to let imagination take control, so read on...

CONTENTS

Olivia Farrington	69	Oliver Hill (10)	111
Annabelle	70	Joshua R	112
Hargun Kaur Poonia (9)	71	Sanjeevan Hayer (10)	113
Olivia Godden (8)	72	Roman Patrick Jameel (10)	114
Thomas Maddison (9)	73		
Oliver Sparrow (9)	74		
Alex Soilleux (9)	75		

Cherry Orchard Primary School, Birmingham

Tilly Lavin (10)	76	Reem Abdaal Hakeem (10)	115
Stanley Ruby (9)	77	Sahil Shubh (9)	116
Tommy Gill (8)	78	Reena Kaur Rai (9)	117
Ryan Singh Sehra (9)	79	Ammara Khan (10)	118
Thomas C	80	Ruqayyah Maryam Sadiq (11)	119
Ria Atwal (10)	81	Inayah Miah Begum (8)	120
Jackson Lee (8)	82	Maryam Qaadhi (8)	121
Lillie Joy Dobson (8)	83	Amira Hussain (11)	122
Kathirvelan Ramaswamy (8)	84	Lilliah Torrens-Pal (11)	123
Harry	85	Rishika Bodapati (9)	124
Eva Bentley (10)	86	Rafan Ali (7)	125
Seanna Dhinsey (9)	87	Haider Naqvi (10)	126
Natalia Anna Harrison (9)	88	Piotr Rajkiewicz (9)	127
Ben Hornigold (10)	89	Zoya Yasser (7)	128
Harrison Lee (9)	90	Skyler Jeffers-Kelly (9)	129
Tillie Kett (9)	91	Jay Karra (8)	130
Jayden Danny Young (9)	92	Niyah Chohan (8)	131
Gurinderjit Singh	93	Jaspreet Chahal (7)	132
Neve Barnett (9)	94	Nikhil Dadral (10)	133
Brooke Judy Leutchford (10)	95	Zofia Kieradlo (8)	134
Joshua William Kelly (8)	96	Amaan Sahonta (11)	135
Beau (8)	97	Yusuf Suhail (8)	136
Aleks Paul Harrison (11)	98	Marah Ali (7)	137
William (8)	99	Ayaan Salim (8)	138
Misha Madeline Chelsea Clews (9)	100		

Great Hollands Primary School, Bracknell

Evie Stewart-Smith (9)	101	Evelyne Jasmine Rose (9)	139
Avneet Kaur Aujla (9)	102	Molly Jennifer Wise (10)	140
Ethan Burke (8)	103	Anshu Sijapati (10)	141
Isobel Puddick (9)	104	Madison Atkinson (11)	142
Dylan	105	Erin Olivia Tobin (11)	143
Mia Rose Vinton (8)	106	Lily-Mae Goode (8)	144
Lenny	107	Ynette Ng Hill (7)	145
Vasian Soldanescu (9)	108	Art Stevens (10)	146
Shaan Rai (10)	109		
Daisy	110		

Isabella Florence Rose (8) 147
Mollie Patrice Waterton (8) 148
Jessica Amy Royle (10) 149
Jamie Barnard Berry (10) 150
Xavi Khan-Sharma (10) 151

Hounslow Heath Junior School, Hounslow

Umathapasvi Kakarlapudi (9) 152
Parag Mittal (10) 153
Shraddha Kori (9) 154
Harim Khan (11) 155
Khushi Puni (10) 156
Eshal Waqas (9) 157
Prisha Kapoor (9) 158
Simionie Galami (10) 159
Rishika Balaji (9) 160
Rihab Belbahi (10) 161
Denis Popescu (10) 162
Zahraa Khan (10) 163
Melissa Rodrigues (11) 164
Shokria Yaqubi (11) 165

Kennoway Primary School, Kennoway

Antoni Lenczowski (7) 166
Lexi Anderson (7) 167
Daniel McGonagle (7) 168
Harley McVey (7) 169
Lucas Jackson Innes (7) 170
Freya Anderson (7) 171
Lewis McGonagle (7) 172
Filip Mis (7) 173
Jimi McIlroy (7) 174
Kaysen Robertson (7) 175
Riley Wilson (7) 176
Cooper McKinstray (7) 177
Marli Auchterlonie (7) 178
Leo Davis (7) 179
Tulisa McBride 180
Macii Fyfe (7) 181
Evan Alistair Michael Cation (7) 182

Kiko (7) 183
Alishba Rehman (7) 184
Jay Pile (7) 185

Potton Lower School, Potton

Billy Albone (8) 186
Alfie Navi (9) 187
Noah Wright (9) 188
Isla Maney (9) 189
Taylor Anthony Hutchison (9) 190
Samuel Hill (8) 191
Joshua Dennis Daniel Oswald (8) 192
Angelo Cucchiara (9) 193
Florence Isabelle Whittaker (9) 194
Florence Thomas (9) 195
Bella Aghera (9) 196
Bethany Kindon (9) 197
Alannah Judd (9) 198

St Peter's Primary Academy, Easton

Tilly Gorgeous Leah Swift (10) 199
Eleanor Crocker (10) 200
Livia Trett (10) 201
Jake Lewis Betts (10) 202
Jacob Wilde (10) 203
Summer-Jade Bevis (9) 204
Olivia Stangroom (10) 205
Isabella Shaw (10) 206
Imogen Easton (9) 207
Eleanor Elsie Miller (9) 208
Imogen Rose Jarvis (9) 209
Safal Neupane (10) 210
Harry James Mills (9) 211
Taylor Osborne (9) 212

St Wystan's School, Repton

Emily Deakin-Jones (8) 213
Eliz Ahmet (10) 214
Teddy Tony Myers-Saunders (8) 215
Grace Amber Thompson (10) 216

Isabel Gavin-Jones (8)   217
Nathan Joseph Bhardwaj (9)   218
Molly Thompson (8)   219
Tilly Lobb (8)   220
Christopher Chenerler (7)   221
Malachi Xavier Easy (8)   222

Watlington Community Primary School, Watlington

Arthur Williams (9)   223
Dylan Whiting (10)   224
Ollie Saw (9)   225
Alex Waterman (9)   226
Harrison Lake Cannon (10)   227

THE STORIES

TOP SECRET

Adventures With Maximus

In a land of heroes lived a family called the Crystalmans. It was Christmas Day.
"Come and open your presents!" shouted Max.
Everyone rushed to the tree but all they found was coal. "Ha! Like your presents?" sneered Max.
"What happened to the presents?" asked Dad.
Max had returned them to Santa.
"Christmas is ruined," sighed Nilly, Max's sister.
Everyone was angry, so angry that they became villains known as The Crystalbads! They wanted their presents so they tried to get hold of Santa.
"Mrs Claus, tell Santa to return our presents now, or else!"
Mrs Claus was very frightened...

Abigail Akinbodunshe (9)

Bursted Wood Primary School, Bexleyheath

Unfair Crocodile

Once upon a time, there was an unfair crocodile. Other animals wanted to go in the watering hole. The unfair crocodile didn't let anyone in. They always wanted a drink of water, but he didn't let anyone drink it. They tried day and night. It was too much. They tried to bribe him; it didn't work. They tried everything, but nothing worked. They even tried acting like his family. It *still* didn't work.

"What should we do?" said Elephant.

"I don't know" said Rhino.

"I know," said Falcon. "Look for our own watering hole and make him jealous."

"Good idea!"

Freddie

Bursted Wood Primary School, Bexleyheath

Skeleton Vs Easter Bunny

Skeleton was just having a peaceful walk when he saw a bad dragon with the Easter bunny in his hand. "Stop! I should call my team," exclaimed the skeleton so he called them. They were there as quick as a flash.

"We should find his lair then get him!"

So they looked around for his lair.

"I have found it! Let's go in." So they went in.

"Got you!" shouted skeleton

"Never!"

"Let's run after him!" shouted skeleton. "We've got you."

Skeleton told Dragon to surrender and he did.

Then Dragon never did a bad thing again.

Roxie Attree (9)

Bursted Wood Primary School, Bexleyheath

The Easiest Case

In a palace, someone stole the royal crown of Europia. Luckily, the queen decided to call Detective Cat, the best detective there ever was. The young detective looked around for clues and found a ginger hair.
"The only ginger-haired cats are my mother and my sister, not forgetting shape-shifter Kate."
She looked around and saw a claw. All she knew was that she couldn't be the thief - she had black hair and no claws. She looked around for fingerprints and found shape-shifting Kate behind the throne! Quickly, the shape-shifter turned into a lion and dropped the mythical, magical crown.

Melissa YaLe An-Curran (9)

Bursted Wood Primary School, Bexleyheath

Pokémon Land!

I flew through the portal. *Where am I? What's happened?* Soon, I knew the answer to these questions: I was in Pokémon Land! I was astonished!

Feeling dizzy, I made my way to what looked like a school. But wait, who was this? A Pokémon? Wow! I looked in my Pokémon encyclopaedia and knew he was Dragonite the Ultra Beast!

Once I got into the school, I met Shan, our friendly headmaster. He gave me my timetable and said with a grin, "You'll have a phenomenal time at this wonderful school!"

"Thanks for this opportunity!" I shouted down the hall.

Amelia Y-J
Bursted Wood Primary School, Bexleyheath

Technology World!

Once upon a time, there were two people called Phoney and Tevy. They were having fun in a park. Their parents were speaking to each other when suddenly, the kids came running down.

"Mummy! There is a new burger coming out today at McDonald's!" said Phoney to his mum.

"Can we go and test it out please?" asked Tevy.

They arrived at McDonald's and they were already screaming. They bought the burger and started eating. Suddenly, Crushey arrived, but Phoney got up and kicked him into another universe! Everybody cheered! They were saved from the Crushey once again!

Louis Nuttall (8)

Bursted Wood Primary School, Bexleyheath

Power Of Charm

William and Charm are best friends. Charm is William's pet pig. They were once walking together in the forest when they saw ants. They growled.

"Charm, let's get them!" said William.

Charm nodded his head.

"Alright, use Fire Fang!" said William.

Then, all of a sudden, a mirage of fireballs shot out of Charm's mouth and destroyed them - but then, in a ball of light, Charm turned into Mega Charm.

"Yeet!" cheered William.

But then they heard a roaring sound. It sounded horrible. It sounded like a call of death. Then they realised that the fight wasn't over yet...

William Wells (9)

Bursted Wood Primary School, Bexleyheath

The Mysterious Board Game!

One day, me and my two friends were playing a game called the animals' forest. We were all nice and cosy sitting on the sofa. I was about to roll the dice. In the blink of an eye, I got into this terrifying world! My friend's faces were shocked!

"Where are we?" shouted Zack.

Suddenly, a scary animal popped up!

"OMG!" exclaimed Lily.

I knew what it was... It was a shark! Behind us, we saw a portal. We jumped in it and we landed back in our cosy home.

"We're back!" screamed intelligent Zack.

We were all really joyful!

Elsie Holland (9)

Bursted Wood Primary School, Bexleyheath

Helping The Town!

One day there was a boy and a girl called Tommy and Lillia. They had superpowers. Tommy's superpower was running and Lillia's power was singing. One day, they heard a massive noise. It sounded like this: "Rrrraaafffddd!"
They went to check it out. There was a troublemaker who made people into troublemakers too! Lillia sang a song and Tommy got the troublemakers all active. They sang a song. "There's no place I'd rather be!"
At first, the troublemaker didn't really like it. After a while, his feet began to tap and he joined in!

Dolcie Harris (8)
Bursted Wood Primary School, Bexleyheath

The Sponge Is Back!

On a normal Bikini Bottom day, SpongeBob came back from his long vacation. When SpongeBob came back to his home, there were some surprises waiting for him. Even though SpongeBob lived in a pineapple, his house was massive. When SpongeBob opened his door, there was a party waiting for him! He and his friends partied all night.

The next morning, Patrick woke SpongeBob up and told him he had a great day planned. It was jellyfishing, SpongeBob's favourite thing to do. They headed over to the jellyfishing court and caught so many jellyfish and had their jam put in sandwiches.

Amber Nash (11)

Bursted Wood Primary School, Bexleyheath

The Missing Jewels

In a tiny, busy town, people were very suspicious. It was just a normal misty, miserable day like always in London. It was so busy in London, crowds screaming, police surrounding. No one knew that two 'normal people' were actually detectives solving a mystery!

Suddenly, *bang! Boom! Bash! Nee-naw, nee-naw, nee-naw!* Police arrived. The detectives said, "Let us in! We can find out who the culprit is!"

But the culprit had already escaped. Soon, the detectives, Cleo and Bob, went home.

The next day, they arrived. They found out the culprit...

Sophie Keen (9)
Bursted Wood Primary School, Bexleyheath

The Place Where Pokémon Live

As I woke up from bed last night, I got sucked through a portal immediately. It was a school where Pokémon learnt their powers - then, one day, Charmander learned his powers (which were electric) and he made everything go *boom!* Pichu came along and tried to defeat Charmander and his power was wind.

The school Pokémon were always misbehaving, then they all learnt their powers at last. They all had a battle, then they nearly all won! Finally, only one remained and then he got really happy cause he won the tournament! They shouted, "Hooray!"

Aiden Fisher
Bursted Wood Primary School, Bexleyheath

The Unique Unicorn

As the unique unicorn stepped out his mansion, his sunglasses shone in the sunlight. In the distance, a small party was going on. As soon as he was there, all the unicorns fled.

"I wonder why they always run away," he sighed.

Suddenly, a small unicorn came up to him. He said, "Are you okay?"

As he turned round, the two were friends instantly. As he approached the village, they gasped at the sight. The unicorn put a red rose on and made people laugh and the unicorn was loved by everyone!

The moral is, don't judge people ever.

Jacob Carter (10)

Bursted Wood Primary School, Bexleyheath

Habhire

Once there lived a killer called Habhire, he was in the papers everywhere for he'd murdered 100 people in his life. He was horrible to people and had no heart, so everyone was terrified of him. Most people didn't know that Habhire's dad was killed when he was only 6 years old, and that's why he killed people - for revenge.

One day, Habhire was shot dead by the police. The people shouted, "Yes, he is dead!" But when the police found out what happened they felt sorry for him, but there was nothing they could do - he was already dead.

Ronnie

Bursted Wood Primary School, Bexleyheath

Space Dinosaurs

I flew through the portal, falling with a *swish* through the air. *Lucky I was wearing a spacesuit!* I thought. *I would have been suffocated.* Anyway, while falling, I spotted a spaceship with a dinosaur in it. Wait... dinosaur? Then I noticed there were dinosaurs on every planet... wow! Then I saw lots of spaceships. One even had a triceratops in it! The triceratops had a crew. This must've meant they escaped from Earth by building a spaceship and surviving on other planets! This definitely meant dinosaurs weren't extinct!

Kemeng Xiong (8)
Bursted Wood Primary School, Bexleyheath

The Sub-Zero Hero

I was inside my hut when there was a bang at the door. Standing outside was a large alien. I was confused. He boomed, "Come to battle with me!"
"How silly! Why should I fight in space?"
"You are of my kind and our galaxy is in trouble! You were sent here as a child."
"Why should I come?" I asked.
"Our planet is in big trouble. An alien species is attacking!"
I refused and shook my head, but he grabbed a sack and kidnapped me! He took me to the spaceship. The engine growled and off we went...

Ramona H
Bursted Wood Primary School, Bexleyheath

The Secrets Of The Nile

The water flowed viciously down the stream. A gun fired close to the vessel, yet the passengers were oblivious to the malicious sound of screaming. There was a shadow lurking by the banks, a reflection of fear. There were footsteps heard on the lower deck, banging and thumping. The captain shivered and hastened towards the phone. Added to the tension was another pair of footsteps. Covered in darkness stood a rather bony and tall man holding a gun in front of him. The captain gasped! Another man knocked the killer off the deck. The captain was safe and he sighed.

Daniel Quinn (11)

Bursted Wood Primary School, Bexleyheath

Haylay's Mission In Space

There Haylay was, standing face to face with an evil alien, her turncoat of an assistant standing close by. She drew out a rocket gun and pointed it at Haylay's heart. Haylay stepped away, panicking, then she saw the black hole. Grinning, Haylay broke into a sprint with the villains following behind her. All of a sudden, she swerved out of the way. Surprisingly, the alien threw his assistant into the black hole!

"Don't worry, she was the leader. I'm Agent B," explained Agent B.

Haylay sighed with relief. It was going to be okay.

Wura Oyabayo (9)

Bursted Wood Primary School, Bexleyheath

How The World Was Made: An Alternate History

Our whole universe was in a hot, dense state; then, nearly fourteen billion years ago, expansion started. It all started with a black hole which sucked in anything that the asteroids made. They tried to merge together to form planets. Two of the asteroids, which were made from flint, hit each other to make fire. They lit up the other asteroids to make the sun. This somehow made a forcefield around it so the Earth could be made safely. Then animals and humans appeared. Restaurants and grocery stores were made of tiny asteroids so that nobody would have to hunt.

Sanjana Shankar (11)
Bursted Wood Primary School, Bexleyheath

Goose Chase

In a small lake, the goose lay, until the worldwide hunter Brandon jumped from the bushes! The goose bolted out of the lake as Brandon ran at it. Soon, Brandon had chased the goose to an abandoned, polluted factory, but when the goose got there, Brandon didn't expect the goose to jump straight into the toxic waste and sink to the bottom! Suddenly, seconds later, the goose jumped out of the waste, nearly tripled in size, and began to run at Brandon with fast, incredible speed! Brandon ran fast as well, thinking he had a chance - but it wasn't enough...

Brandon Thomas West (10)
Bursted Wood Primary School, Bexleyheath

The Missing Gift

One day, Lilly and Amily were opening their calendar. It was the 24th, but Lilly had a feeling that her present would not get delivered. The time had come and the girls went to bed.

It was the next morning and the only presents that were there were Amily's. Lilly said that she had to go and find hers.

They found a clue. It said *702*. That was the door number for the house that stole it! There it was, a whole pile of gifts.

Finally, the girls went home and had a happy Christmas.

"Yay," Lilly said, "a phone!"

Mylah Brown (10)
Bursted Wood Primary School, Bexleyheath

The Ruined But Fine Candy Land

Once upon a time, there was a world of unicorns that lived in Candy Land. The most famous unicorn was the queen. One day, while the unicorns were playing and having fun, a dark ship covered Candy Land, then the Devil came. He was wrecking all the candy and ruining the chocolate milk! Unicorns started panicking. They couldn't use their magic because it wasn't that powerful.

Then the Queen went face to face with the Devil. The Queen knew that the Devil wouldn't stand a chance against her, so she used all her might and a shining beam hit him!

Sadie Jayne Hardwick (8)

Bursted Wood Primary School, Bexleyheath

Shapes

As I was flying through the great Atlantic Ocean, my voice monitor to an unknown place started going crazy. The propellors were failing to spin, so I began to worry. I thought I was having a nightmare until my hands started moving and my feet were shaking vigorously. I then found myself in a completely parallel world. On my arrival, I revealed an intergalactic secret. This was a myth in my reality, the Tirpod Legion and the never-ending war against the Globnort Army. I then realised I needed to escape this crazy intergalactic world before I met my fate...

Oscar Duggan (10)
Bursted Wood Primary School, Bexleyheath

Murder Town

Deep in the shadows of the town in 1882, there wasn't a single person around except the builders. They were planting some giant microphones to warn people about the war.

Suddenly, a family came running out of the house saying, "KillerX is in our house!"

So the builders called Detective Pikachu and his Pokémon police force - then Slade came out. They were surrounded by the police. The best friends Slade and KillerX tried to run. The Pokémon had a giant net and threw it. They were caught!

"Yes! I completed the level on my brand new game!"

Lauren Care (10)

Bursted Wood Primary School, Bexleyheath

Dream Mystery

It was dark. The night was dull and the smallest light was coming from the east. A player, Battlenitro999, felt an uneasy, paranoid feeling coming upon him. BN9 (which he wanted to be known as) was perplexed why it was so dark.
Bam! A spirit hovered over him. BN9 activated his weapon. As he was a fire and light elemental, he tried to break the darkness. It only grew. With sorrow on his devastating face, he left as a failure. The spirit came to destroy him...
"Oh no!"
Then he found out it wasn't real - it was just a dream!

Oluwarojoayo Senbore (10)
Bursted Wood Primary School, Bexleyheath

Candy Cane Lane!

I stepped into the wonderful land called Candy Cane Lane. I wanted to eat the candy, but it said, "No eating the candy!"
I was so sad. When I walked down Candy Cane Lane, I could smell the wonderful candy canes and the melting marshmallows melting in the sun.
Then, when no one was looking, I ate the delicious-looking candy canes and the beautiful-looking marshmallows!
But then there was no beautiful candy left in Candy Cane Lane anymore. Then I hung tinsel everywhere instead of beautiful, fabulous candy canes and melted marshmallows.

Lucy
Bursted Wood Primary School, Bexleyheath

The Magical Letter

Once upon a time there was a friendly girl called Amy, who was the best in her class at training horses. One evening, whilst grooming her horse Lily at the stables, she heard a 'whoosh' and in her hand she was holding a letter inviting her to a magical horse show.

"The show is very soon so we need to get practising Lily," Amy said to her horse. And so they practised and practised.

The day came and Amy went to buy some treats to calm Lily's nerves. When Amy went to check on Lily, she screamed... Lily was gone!

Ruby Brown
Bursted Wood Primary School, Bexleyheath

The Apocalpse

In a laboratory deep underground, the black virus escaped and it turned into the apocalypse. There were only a few survivors with weapons left. The zombies had increased from one to a hundred million. The zombies had taken over most of the countries in the world. They had taken over every country you could think of, like England, Spain, France, Russia, China, Japan, Australia, Mexico... No country was safe in the apocalypse. All military personnel were wiped out and all the police as well. Scientists were working on a cure for the dead plague virus...

Callum Ayres

Bursted Wood Primary School, Bexleyheath

It's Christmas!

There once was a young girl on Christmas Eve. She ran in the garden with a Christmas grin on her rosy red face. In the corner of her eye, she saw something glowing. She ran to see what it was! The little girl tripped over a log and...
woosh! Suddenly, she was in a sparkling winter wonderland! She opened her eyes and there appeared a blushing face with a bushy white beard.

"Ho ho ho!" said Santa.

"Santa!"

"Here's your present!"

"Yay!"

She opened it and a little elf popped out!

"Thank you!"

"Merry Christmas!"

Emma Pollock (10)
Bursted Wood Primary School, Bexleyheath

Nazis Are In Control

I go through a mysterious portal and already my mouth opens. I see my city in flames. I see a big group of people bowing to a man with a small, bad moustache above his mouth. There are soldiers, who I think are German, pointing guns at innocent people!
I go over to the people and say, "What's going on?"
They don't reply - then I see a soldier coming up to me and saying, "Where were you? You should have been here an hour ago! This is your last chance!"
I quickly say, "Sorry!"
That was close...

Jacob Waghorn (7)
Bursted Wood Primary School, Bexleyheath

Missing Jewels

"Breaking news: Crown Jewels stolen. A detective was called last night and is searching the neighbourhood. Who could the culprit be?"

The detective knocked on a door and asked some questions.

The man said, "Okay, okay, I did it! Just leave me alone. Take the jewels, I don't care anymore."

So the detective took the jewels to the police and the man was arrested for ten years straight. The Queen was given back her Crown Jewels and was very happy. The detective got an award and was very happy. The man wasn't.

Keira Murrell (9)
Bursted Wood Primary School, Bexleyheath

The Very Mean Bully!

Once upon a time, there was a girl called Jemma and a mean boy called Ryan. Ryan was always mean to Jemma. Jemma didn't know why Ryan was always mean to her.

One day, Ryan was being so bossy and was treating her as a slave, but when she tried to go without him looking, she always got caught. Then a pretty, brave mummy unicorn appeared. She stood in front of the girl, but Jemma thought, *unicorns can't talk... How will she save me?* But then the unicorn spoke!

"Stop treating her like a slave, otherwise I will kill you!"

Lyla Lennon (8)
Bursted Wood Primary School, Bexleyheath

The House Of Doom

I walked through the door and a spell hit me. My fingers turned transparent and a dreadful moaning noise occurred. It dragged through my brain as I strolled through the door and into the library.

Then, when my hand felt a handle, I pulled down and something small came out. I went ghost-like so the scroll hit the floor and it read, 'This house is haunted. The longer you stay, you will turn into a ghost and never see light...'

When I felt my body, shock appeared. It was almost complete! I ran, but the door wouldn't let me out...

Hattie Pigott-Denyer (11)
Bursted Wood Primary School, Bexleyheath

The Last Seat Of The Table

Once in Camelot, King Arthur had one seat left at his round table, so he needed a knight brave, strong and mighty - but little did he know that there was a boy who was strong and mighty.
The boy, who was on an adventure, found the mighty castle of King Arthur. The king spotted the young lad. Suddenly, a knight came with a sword and tried to kill the boy! The knight missed. The boy killed the knight.
King Arthur asked, "What's your name?"
The boy answered, "I'm Hester."
The boy got knighted and finished the round table.

Lewis Hutchings (9)
Bursted Wood Primary School, Bexleyheath

The Mystery Canvas

Martha walked through the dark alleyway and suddenly, a shadow appeared! For one reason, she could tell that the person was a thief: they were holding a canvas and there were police sirens in the distance! Loud footsteps came closer, closer and closer behind Martha... but all it was was Jemma! Jemma was her friend and she told her everything. They chased after the thief. After a while, they got lost... until they saw the man's face. They noticed it was Martha's uncle! She was confused. Her parents normally told her anything and everything...

Leah Adegabi (9)
Bursted Wood Primary School, Bexleyheath

Crazy Christmas!

I stepped into the portal and I arrived in Christmas Land! I saw two Santas but one looked evil and one looked nice. Also, they were fighting and I just realised I could fly so I went up to see what was wrong.

"Hey you, nice Santa, why are you giving toys instead of cannons?" asked the evil Santa.

"Because cannons are bad and they need good presents and toys," replied the nice Santa.

I asked what was wrong, but the evil Santa got his cannon out and fired the nice Santa and he flung out of the entire world.

Lola Cotta (8)

Bursted Wood Primary School, Bexleyheath

The Flying Person

There was a boy known as normal Norman, who walked everywhere he went.

One day when walking around London, Norman felt a strange tingling feeling all through his body. He started to float into the air, but got scared, so he tried to grab onto a wall. When this didn't work, he hovered higher and higher in the air, until he was as tall as The Shard. Norman got stuck on top of it. He saw people down below, shouting, "Do you need help?" Norman felt that he'd be stuck up there forever, but luckily the police saved him.

Taylor Barrow (9)
Bursted Wood Primary School, Bexleyheath

The Invasion Of Christmas

It was Christmas night and Santa had all the presents ready to deliver. He jumped onto his sleigh and put the presents behind him. He sang Jingle Bells on the way.

Suddenly, above the sleigh, there was a light. It shone above the sleigh, then the sleigh got caught! The light pulled the sleigh into another sleigh. Father Christmas had a look. It was his evil brother! Mrs Christmas got a pudding gun and shot Evil Christmas and Christmas was saved as quick as a flash! Evil Christmas got hypnotised by the pudding gun he had made himself!

Derin-Dijan Sarioglu (9)
Bursted Wood Primary School, Bexleyheath

The Mermaid's Kingdom

One day, Olivia skipped along a meadow and found a lake. She was told it had mermaids inside it, so she jumped in! Suddenly, she found herself drowning. A mermaid then saw her and grabbed Olivia, then took her to a mermaid kingdom where all mermaids lived...

Once Olivia woke up, she found herself in a mermaid kingdom. She thanked the creature and became good friends with all of the others. She jumped out the lake and went home, but before that, she gave one last smile to the lake and nobody else ever knew about her mermaid secret.

Kimryn Thumber (9)
Bursted Wood Primary School, Bexleyheath

The Climbing Pixie!

Once, there was a pixie who lived in a bauble on a Christmas tree. Every Christmas, Robby and his family got the tree out and put it up. The pixie's name was Tinsel. Tinsel loved Christmas.
One day, Robby knocked Tinsel's bauble off the tree and it smashed.
"No!" squeaked Tinsel. She was devastated. Robby threw the bauble in the bin and ran to his room. Tinsel knew what to do, so she climbed to the top of the tree. A lovely fairy lived in the star. Tinsel swung her tiny leg over the nearest branch. The star was shining...

Nancy Haynes (9)
Bursted Wood Primary School, Bexleyheath

A Locked Door

I took a step forward and I found myself appearing in a desert. As my eyes adjusted, a colossal boat anchored itself. Pirates emerged. I took a step back and found myself on the floor. I looked in front. I tripped over a treasure chest as the pirates were getting closer. I panicked and hid behind an oak tree. I got over my fear after a while and stepped out from behind the tree, but the treasure chest was gone! That's when I knew I could never leave the house again because something would get taken from my treasured belongings...

Grace Matthews (9)
Bursted Wood Primary School, Bexleyheath

Back Into A World Of Different

I stepped through the portal, not knowing what I was going to find. Confused, I looked around. It looked the same as the world I'd left... but out of a cloud of volcano ash came a furious dinosaur! It charged at me and I realised I was in a straw nest. There were three large Creme Eggs inside. Not thinking, I leapt out of the nest into an ash-cloud, extremely hurting myself - but there was no time to stop. Quickly, the dinosaur began to run. In the distance, the dinosaur charged. More frightened than ever, I ran to stay alive...

Imogen Martin (8)
Bursted Wood Primary School, Bexleyheath

The New Goddess

Once upon a time, there were twelve gods and goddesses. All of the goddesses were expecting a new girl goddess from the goddess Aphrodite. She was going to be the prettiest of the lot, people were saying.

For days, nothing happened, until one night, Aphrodite was holding a peculiar baby. She was peculiar because she had the most beautiful face, a horn, a mermaid tail and a pair of fairy wings. Everyone was relieved.

After weeks, she was seen by Zeus, the king of all the gods. Aphrodite was now married to the king forever.

Dakota Leigh Everest-Hicks (9)

Bursted Wood Primary School, Bexleyheath

Bouncing Pug Land

I went into a portal and I was a pug, then I was bouncing up and down. I wondered what was going on. I was on a trampoline. They were everywhere!

Then I saw a human. I blinked and he was a pug! I turned around and everyone was a pug. They were continuously bouncing. We were all uncontrollably bouncing everywhere! We were on uncontrollable trampolines!

I bounced into a pug and we fell over. I said sorry at the same as him.

He said, "Do you want to be friends? It will be great!"

I said, "Yes."

Lewis Hurst (8)

Bursted Wood Primary School, Bexleyheath

The Dinosaur Arctic

I wake up, feeling dazed. I move my arm. Something is just not right. I reluctantly open my eyes as I hear coos. Finally, my eyes adjust to the sunlight and I make out the features of some small dinosaurs standing in front of the radiant sun. Suddenly, a clamorous roar makes me shoot up like a bullet. There is a vast forest stretched out beyond me. The dinosaurs dart into the undergrowth, followed by me, just in time to escape a colossal allosaur lumbering towards us. We are safe. I take in what just happened. A whole new world...

Teo Abramovich (9)
Bursted Wood Primary School, Bexleyheath

The Surprise

I had just come home from school.
"Mum!"
No reply. It was dark, almost too dark. I went to my bed. It was a bit messy, not like I had left it. "Someone has been in here," I muttered under my breath, and whoever it was was still there. I cautiously leaned into my mum's room. No one. I was alone...
"Surprise! Happy birthday!"
Somebody popped out of my bed, another out of my wardrobe!
Phew! I had the surprise of my life, but then... oh no! I realised it wasn't my birthday. This was not my family! Oops!

Aggeliki Mirza (10)
Bursted Wood Primary School, Bexleyheath

Mythical Marvellous Myth

I woke up and found myself in a gigantic world of wonders. Suddenly, I found a unicorn with a horn so sparkly I couldn't believe my eyes! I was intimidated. My heart missed a beat. Then I got really happy because I got to ride the unicorn! Then I heard a scream saying, "Help me!"
I ran as quickly as a flash. I saw a big building full of unicorns. They were the most beautiful things that I had ever seen. There was someone stuck in the middle and they looked terrified. They were half woman and half unicorn!

Paige Crouch (8)
Bursted Wood Primary School, Bexleyheath

Time Travelling!

One Stone Age day, there lived a girl called Oug. She was going hunting. When she was crossing the forest, Oug got lost and found a portal off the path. The portal had lots of swirls and it looked interesting so she walked through it...

It wasn't the Stone Age anymore! There was flying cars and flying UFOs. She realised that she was in the year 5012AD! Also, there were asteroids shooting down from space. The portal was gone! She had to live in this weird, futuristic and ruined world from now and then onwards forever...

Senuth

Bursted Wood Primary School, Bexleyheath

Unicorn

I stepped into my garden and there I saw a girl with a unicorn in her backpack. I mean, what? Then I saw houses and roads with unicorns wandering up and down, some with pink hair, purple hair and so many more colours! Underneath the leaves lay the queen unicorn. I was so nervous, but I said, "Hello, I love unicorns and I have always been admiring you, but I have to say bye." I walked into my house. My mum was waiting for me. I had my dinner and climbed into bed "Night night!" I love unicorns!

Faye (8)
Bursted Wood Primary School, Bexleyheath

Christmas Is Coming

On Christmas Eve, George was putting his cookies for Santa on the side of the coffee table. He hung up his Christmas stocking and got ready for bed. He fell asleep but got woken up by a noise. It sounded like bells. George slowly got out of bed and opened the dinosaur-covered curtains. He looked outside and could not believe his small brown eyes. He saw something amazing, the best thing he'd ever seen in this life. He could not wait to tell people that he saw Father Christmas! George was over the moon! He was very, very happy.

Hayley Maddison (10)
Bursted Wood Primary School, Bexleyheath

Devil's Midnight

I was in a dark room with no one inside. There were ghosts lurking and doors creaking and then the lightning struck me! I was dressed like a devil. I realised I could fly! I had a trident of dark magic and horns! I could never believe it!

I looked at the time. *Oh, it's past my bedtime*, I thought. *It's midnight!*

Anyway, then my power struck me and I roamed Earth in my evil ways. Then I thought, *will I ever go back home? I hope my parents don't find out...*
Evil ruled Earth.

Serin Hassan (9)
Bursted Wood Primary School, Bexleyheath

The Enchanting Magical Forest

There is a unicorn called Summer. She goes into an enchanting forest, then she finds a candy house, so she has a look. It belongs to a good witch. The witch thinks Summer is very cute, so she decides to keep her. The witch's name is Ellie. Ellie gives her some candy and an Oreo milkshake.

Summer decides she wants a nap, so Ellie makes her a bed. Summer has an hour's nap, then she starts playing all afternoon! Then they go to the enchanted lake and drink the magical water and have the best time of their lives!

Millie

Bursted Wood Primary School, Bexleyheath

The Attack Of The Superhero Vs Doll!

I stepped into the portal and closed my eyes and, after ten minutes, I opened my eyes again. I realised I was on Mars. Good job I knew all about planets! Mars was very strange. All of a sudden, one doll leg just thumped beside me and another doll leg thumped on the other side of me! I didn't realise a doll was standing above me. I wanted to go back home and I said to myself, "I really want to go home..."

But all of a sudden, I saw a superhero and a doll fighting, and at that moment, the superhero won!

Jessie Tuersley (8)
Bursted Wood Primary School, Bexleyheath

Mercy Medusa Mercy

Once upon a time, there was a monster, Medusa. People in the jungle were terrified of her and normally didn't go out in the jungle, so most of them starved to death...
One day, a boy about six years old called Josh wanted to explore the jungle, but his parents said no. So, one night, Josh jumped out of the window and went to explore the jungle. On the way, Josh heard a hissing sound - then he turned around and saw Medusa! Luckily, Josh came prepared and had a shield and a sword - but Josh had turned to stone...

Lowenna Myrna Bainbridge (9)
Bursted Wood Primary School, Bexleyheath

The Adventure Of The New Land

There once was a boy called Tim who went to discover some caves. Hours later, he found a big cave that light was coming out of. Tim went in and found a portal. Tim found something saying, *Make a wish and go through the portal.* He thought of a wish and went in...

Two minutes later, he woke up on a golf course. He said, "How has this happened? Cool!"

This was his dream that came true!

"I should play golf!"

Twenty-four hours later, he fell asleep and woke up in his house...

Harry Fryer (10)
Bursted Wood Primary School, Bexleyheath

The Missing Gang

Once upon a time, there was a missing gang and they were called Team Rocket. They were snatching Pokémon, so the detective went to find them. On the way, he met a girl called Misty and a boy called Brock.

One day, they saw a man who wanted to challenge them and they won with creatures called Pikachu and Zekrom.

Three hours later, the detective saw a bad Pokémon, so they then captured it and turned it good, but that was a distraction! Finally, they found Team Rocket and then they were imprisoned.

Jack O'Doherty (10)

Bursted Wood Primary School, Bexleyheath

The Life Of A Jack Russell

I stepped through the bright portal slowly. I started seeing parts of Trampoline Land. There were dogs roaming the land and I was one! Quickly, I ran to see other pugs, Jack Russels, chihuahuas and corgis. Slowly, I became more excited, but I felt they were keeping a secret from me...

One night, the other dogs went to a field. I was scared. I thought they were going to throw me out of their land, but no, they did not. They were making sure nobody saw them turning into humans! Who knows - maybe humans are dogs?

Emily Quinn
Bursted Wood Primary School, Bexleyheath

Surprise!

As I lay on my sunbed, I thought to myself, *it is nice to have some time off!* but then a monster appeared! Suddenly, I jumped up and started chasing it. It went all over the garden and jumped on the bench. My hands gripped against its fur until it ran into the bushes. I went into my house all prepared. I got some peanut butter and some chocolate. I laid it against the bushes while waiting carefully. Suddenly, there was a crunch! I looked over with my hands ready. There, jumping out in surprise, was my cat!

Claudia Kamara (10)
Bursted Wood Primary School, Bexleyheath

On The Moon

I jumped through the portal to another world. The floor was sand and there was an alien - then I realised I was in space!

The alien said, "Why are you here?"

I said, "How can you speak human when you are an alien?"

"No, you are an alien," said the alien.

I calmed him down by saying, "Let's just say we are both aliens."

"Okay," agreed the alien happily.

I jumped back through the portal and went back home where everything was normal.

Charlie Walker

Bursted Wood Primary School, Bexleyheath

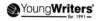

Mystery On Bullstrat Road

As I hopped through the portal, I fell into a narrow hall. It was pitch-black except for a woman (Miranda) next to me.

"What do I do?" asked Miranda.

A mysterious mist swirled around her. Suddenly, she fell dead!

I wondered, "What's going on?"

The smell of blood floated around the room. The atmosphere was tense. I walked to the switch and turned on the light. A murderer stood there with a knife! I jumped through the portal before I got hurt.

Phew! That was so close!

Isabella P (9)
Bursted Wood Primary School, Bexleyheath

Shark Land Chase

I stepped inside a bright portal, then I found myself in Shark Land! There were different types of shark, including the speed shark and the fin shark.
Suddenly, the fin and speed sharks started chasing me! I swam and swam and swam and swam until I got tired, but I still swam. Unfortunately, the speed shark was still swimming. The fin shark passed out! The king of sharks joined the chase. He was double the size of all the sharks (except from the big shark)!
I swam back into the bright, colourful portal...

Edward (8)
Bursted Wood Primary School, Bexleyheath

Simplifyer

One day in the town of Yeesville, a superhero named The Simplifyer was resting in his HQ when he heard the phone ring. It was a call to help the citizens of Hamley from a villain named Soul Slayer. He was on it right away! He sat on his special chair and pressed the eject button and flew through the roof. He typed in 'Hamley' on his teleportation system and shook it for five seconds and then he was in Hamley! He saw the monster and jumped really high and sliced his head off. That was his wonderful mission!

Fraser Parsons
Bursted Wood Primary School, Bexleyheath

The Mystical Island

Once, there was a magical island full of fairies, unicorns and talking animals and they all lived happily. One day, out of nowhere, a meteor hit the island, causing it to rot. Luckily everyone had evacuated and went underground. The problem was they could not go to the surface. One of the fairies could not find a solution but everyone begged her to think of one. Finally she found a way - she would make it rain enchanted water and save the world; there was only one problem, she couldn't find her wand...

Raninderjit
Bursted Wood Primary School, Bexleyheath

Abominations From [Unknown]

I dramatically leapt into the portal, not knowing anything about it or what was in store. I woke up in a strange dimension. The first thing looked really... strange... It was tall, skinny, covered in blood and just spooky in general. It laid its blood-curdling hands on my shoulder, and screeched, "Follow me, mortal human!"

He led me outside and I saw a land of abominations from [Unknown]! What? That looked like a cyclops coconut! It started shooting blazing demon skulls!

"Argh...!"

Keon Lucas (9)
Bursted Wood Primary School, Bexleyheath

The Monkey Dancer And The Bills

One day there was a monkey and it stared me in the eyes. Suddenly, it started dancing, then everything went black...

I woke up in the Monkey Temple and I saw monkeys surrounding me, then... they started dancing. My hands were growing hair and even my face was... then I smelt something. It was a banana! I ran and ran until I got to it. It was a man dressed as a banana... I pounced!

Suddenly, I woke up with a smooshed banana on my face and bills everywhere. I then realised it was a dream the whole time.

Augustas (10)
Bursted Wood Primary School, Bexleyheath

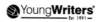

The Big Mistake

Once, there was a world with a river where a mermaid lived. There was a cave where a dragon lived. There was a happy thoughtful unicorn. One day the mermaid called Sofia went to buy a mug with the unicorn called Sparkles. When they came back Sparkles wanted to show Sofia her house Sofia said, "I'll quickly go and put my mug away." When the dragon saw it he wanted to hold it. So the dragon ran away with it and when he ran he dropped the mug. He was so afraid to tell Sofia that he hid away forever.

Tallulah Richens (8)
Bursted Wood Primary School, Bexleyheath

The Little Boy's Wish

Once upon a time, a little boy loved Xmas and he wanted to go to the North Pole. Then, one day, he saw Santa and Santa said, "I am going to bring you to the North Pole."

The little boy was so excited that he jumped out of bed and he ran into the sleigh. At last, they got to the North Pole and he saw the nine reindeer: Rudolph, Comet, Cupid, Donner, Prancer, Dancer, Dasher, Blitzen and Vixen. They both jumped back in the sleigh and flew back to the little boy's bedroom and he went to sleep.

Mason Mulvihill (8)
Bursted Wood Primary School, Bexleyheath

The World Of Candy

I was just having a nice little snooze. I woke up and everything was different. I went outside, looked at my house, and all of it was made out of candy! Actually, the whole entire world was made out of candy! Even worse, I had to go to school that day. Even the people were candy. I didn't like it. I kept on saying in my head, *I want to go home now. I don't like this place at all. Pretty please can I go home now? I'm begging you.*

Then something weird happened and I went back home.

Sienna Wade (8)

Bursted Wood Primary School, Bexleyheath

Year 1955

The year was 2019. Delilah moved into her new home and got lost. She found a room with no light coming out from it. She tried to bash the door down, which worked, but she ended up with lots of bruises.

Delilah was scared about this room. She entered the room. A light shone! She saw a machine. She walked closer and, all of a sudden, she got sucked in!

She woke up and found herself in 1955! She even found her mother as a baby!

She suddenly fell over and woke up back in 2019. What a weird day!

Olivia Farrington
Bursted Wood Primary School, Bexleyheath

Sparkle Trot's Magic

I once woke up and I saw a lot of sweets and unicorns. I quickly got dressed and I saw my best unicorn friend, Sparkle Trots. We began to walk over the rainbow, but then Sparkle Trots saw a reindeer. She started to run away all over the place. They both got lost in the magical forest... After a while, I had to go to find them. I looked and looked, but I still couldn't find them.
The next day, around 8am, I found them both. I told Sparkle Trots that reindeer were okay and we were all friends.

Annabelle

Bursted Wood Primary School, Bexleyheath

Christmas Eve

It was Christmas Eve and this little girl called Poppy had put milk and cookies down next to the chimney and went to bed. She was so excited to open her presents that she just couldn't sleep. She slowly snuck downstairs as fast as she could. Poppy waited for Santa to come, but Santa didn't come and she was so tired...

As she was sleeping, she heard this jingling sound and she thought it was Rudolph, but it wasn't. Now she knew Santa wouldn't come, so she was so upset all night...

Hargun Kaur Poonia (9)
Bursted Wood Primary School, Bexleyheath

The Mystery Of Christmas

There was once a season called Christmas and everybody loved it. It was a season where good children got their presents. The naughty children got coal for Christmas, but only a small amount of children were naughty in the world.

One cold night, Santa came, but he only had Rudolph on his sleigh because all of them had a cold but Rudolph. Santa and Rudolph set off in the sleigh and gave some presents to the good children only.

"I wonder how the other reindeers got sick..." said Santa.

Olivia Godden (8)
Bursted Wood Primary School, Bexleyheath

The Day Roger Federer Played Rafael Nadal

I walked through the portal and I was Roger Federer! I went to play Rafael Nadal in a very tough match, but sadly, halfway through, my racket turned evil. It even gobbled up somebody! I said to their family I was very sorry, but they didn't forgive me.

So, in my next match, I got Nadal to hit the ball as hard as he could at my racket so it would smash. Thankfully, it worked and it broke, so I got a new racket and it was perfectly fine. I played Nadal again and, even better, I won the match!

Thomas Maddison (9)

Bursted Wood Primary School, Bexleyheath

The Land Of The Sun And Moon Zombie Apocalypse

On a hot day at the desert, Metal Ninja went to the dark side of the world, then he saw graves. After a while, a hand pushed out of the ground! Metal Ninja knew the zombie apocalypse was there, so he quickly ran past them before they could erupt from the ground - but it was too late. The zombies were coming towards him. He knew what he had to do: he had to fight them.

After a long and tiring fight, Metal Ninja saw even more zombies were coming, so he ran as quick as the Flash into the sunlight.

Oliver Sparrow (9)

Bursted Wood Primary School, Bexleyheath

The Kitchen

One cold, stormy night, a boy went into a dark, creepy castle. He went into a kitchen and opened a cupboard. A creepy doll jumped out of it! The boy looked behind him and the doors slammed shut. The doll had two sharp knives. The boy tried to run, but the doll was guarding the door. The boy grabbed some knives and threw them at the doll. The doll ducked and the knives missed him. The doll threw a knife at the boy. He got hit and fell to the ground and the doll walked off back into the cupboard...

Alex Soilleux (9)
Bursted Wood Primary School, Bexleyheath

The Worst Day!

One mysterious day, a girl named Emma opened a book by David Walliams and, when she opened the book, there was a portal swirling around and she accidentally fell into it! Everything was dizzy, but as her eyes adjusted, she saw that she was in a weird place. When she saw that it said Tudor, she got out her phone and saw no bars, no wi-fi, no anything! She screamed so loudly you could hear her from Madagascar. Someone came up to her and asked what was wrong. She looked around again and shivered...

Tilly Lavin (10)
Bursted Wood Primary School, Bexleyheath

Drowned!

A young, normal boy in a normal world was in the desert looking for a drink. He had been looking for it for a long while now. He thought, *if the world was water, I could drink it all.*
All of a sudden, the world was drowned in water! He started drowning, so he swam all the way up, then he thought, *I can travel the world!* so he did! He got back and he was very thirsty, so he drank it all. He never ever needed a drink ever again, then he lived happily ever after like normal.

Stanley Ruby (9)
Bursted Wood Primary School, Bexleyheath

The God Of Fire Has Returned

The God of Fire had returned. The devil leapt from the ground and destroyed three helicopters in a row. They were falling to the ground. As they were falling, they were burning and the devil was killing the soldiers and the pilots with his axe, and then he jumped out the window of the helicopter and landed on the ground to find out that there was a zombie apocalypse! He had to kill all of the zombies before night or the ultimate zombie king would arise from the ground and attack him. He did it!

Tommy Gill (8)
Bursted Wood Primary School, Bexleyheath

The Missing Explorer

I built a magical time machine that would take me back to the future. I got into the cramped machine and pressed the glowing button - then a shake happened. I opened the time machine door and there were dinosaurs everywhere! I didn't know what to do! I went to them and they roared. I ran to the time machine to take me into 2019, but it didn't work. Dinosaurs were running to me faster than Usain Bolt, then stone men came running to me! I was screaming so much! What was going to happen to me...?

Ryan Singh Sehra (9)
Bursted Wood Primary School, Bexleyheath

Dragons Now

I stepped into the colourful portal and, as I got out, I realised that, all around me, it was like my lovely world but with scary dragons! I went into a rocky home where I could hide. I came out into the wild and a frightening dragon was looking at me, ready to eat me for supper! Then the horrible chase began. I ran across roads and into a tall building, but still he was chasing me. His breath smelt like rotten eggs! It made me feel sick. Then I got away as a helicopter carried me back home.

Thomas C
Bursted Wood Primary School, Bexleyheath

Adventure Of The Girl!

One sunny summer's day, a young girl lived called Zoe. She had a mum called Chloe and a dad called James. The girl had a brother and a sister. They all lived together in the same house - then, one bright day, Zoe, the young girl, asked to go to the park and her mum said, "Of course."
When Zoe left the house, she walked. When the girl got to the park, she found a boy sitting on the bench, lonely. Then, once the girl had talked to the boy, they went back to Zoe's house.

Ria Atwal (10)
Bursted Wood Primary School, Bexleyheath

Santa Claus

Once upon a time, a boy aged seven loved Christmas. He even wanted to be Santa Claus when he was older! He helped his mum put up the Christmas tree and the decorations. He loved helping people and there was also a fake competition about who would be Santa Claus when they were older. A lot of people thought he would be Santa Claus when he was older because he was a really kind, caring boy and the real Santa Claus at that moment was just like that. He told a lot of people he loved Christmas!

Jackson Lee (8)
Bursted Wood Primary School, Bexleyheath

The Super-Horse

In a place far away, there was a super-horse who lived in the basement of a castle. She saw a girl with snakes as her hair. She walked towards the door and everybody was frozen. She found out that they had spoken to the girl and, if she didn't like what they said, she froze them with her icy look. She knew she had to do something, so she went outside to get a big, heavy stone to defeat the girl with. The super-horse ran at the girl with the stone in her hand and knocked the girl out!

Lillie Joy Dobson (8)
Bursted Wood Primary School, Bexleyheath

Missing Santa

It was bright as the moonlight shone on the ground in the peaceful North Pole - but the elves noticed something, Santa was gone! It was a disaster!

The elf detective came. He was known as Elf Ective! The mission to solve the disappearance of Santa began. The elves began to calm down and cheer for the almighty Elf Ective!

Elf Ective began to search for clues. He slowly started walking to Santa's grotto. Santa wasn't there, but there was a note made out of green card...

Kathirvelan Ramaswamy (8)

Bursted Wood Primary School, Bexleyheath

Stepping Through A Portal

I stepped through a portal and turned into a monster! I had superpowers and I could fly. Also, I could shoot lasers out of my eyes and could shoot really sharp feathers. I could chase people everywhere they went so they wouldn't escape. I had wings, so when I flapped them, I blew people really far away. I had super strength, which meant I could throw cars. I was invincible and bulletproof. I wasn't very good at using my new powers, so I practised and got it so I was good at it!

Harry
Bursted Wood Primary School, Bexleyheath

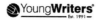

Sweet Dreams

The moon shone through the open windows. The frozen air pinched at my skin. The shadows that lurked in my room had suddenly risen from the deep darkness of the hall. I awoke with a jolt and I heard a whisper. It hissed at me. It dragged me out of my bed and lured me to the attic. I had no choice; I had to follow it. A thin, bony hand clasped my wrist and lifted me into the air! A powerful wind took me in its grip, then... The blazing sunlight burst through the curtains. It was a dream!

Eva Bentley (10)
Bursted Wood Primary School, Bexleyheath

The Mysterious Girl

As I walked near the stream, I had a seat on the bench in the forest. I looked at the beautiful glowing stars and the lovely glowing moon. As I was looking, the bush made a crackling noise. I stared at the bush and saw a little girl. The girl had the blackest hair I had ever seen. She had the most lovely glowing green eyes. She also had a blue gown on with glittering blue matching shoes.
But there was not just a little girl, but a small, little brown dog who had the same eyes...

Seanna Dhinsey (9)
Bursted Wood Primary School, Bexleyheath

The Goddess Squirrel

I was sucked through a portal. I was a normal human, but then my tail started to grow as big as a squirrel's! I arrived at this mystical island. There were humans and animals.

I met this animal talking like a robot! It was saying, "Welcome to Goddess Animal Land." It never left me alone. It said I was going to turn into an animal, and I did!

I arrived at magic practice. I was so nervous, but my friend from school cheered me up. She was half puma, half human!

Natalia Anna Harrison (9)
Bursted Wood Primary School, Bexleyheath

Murder Mystery

One moment I'm on a trampoline, and then I'm in the sky, fighting, looking for dangerous people. I'm looking for a man who stole a lot of cookies. The man's hiding in a long maze. The robber's name is Blaze. He is a fat man who robs a lot. I fly right above the maze, searching for Blaze. He is wearing a red and orange suit. I see a red toe peering out of a bush, then I land straight on the rocks. I see Blaze and start to attack him. He's knocked out and the police are coming...

Ben Hornigold (10)
Bursted Wood Primary School, Bexleyheath

The Superhero

A kid crept into a portal. It was filled with aliens! Santa was giving presents to everyone while the aliens were taking the presents! They were trying to ruin Christmas!

It was all up to the kid. He followed the aliens until they went to sleep. The boy took the presents, giving them to the right children. All the adults cheered with happiness. Christmas was saved by the superhero kid!

The boy went back into the portal. The aliens were furious! They wanted revenge...

Harrison Lee (9)

Bursted Wood Primary School, Bexleyheath

Puppy?

I stepped into a dark house, not knowing what I'd see. I closed my eyes as I stepped in the house. When I was in, I saw a puppy walking a puppy! I saw puppy school. I couldn't believe my eyes! My heart was beating so, so, so fast. My life flashed before my eyes. The puppies all came over to me and landed on top of me and made me fall over. I tried to go back through the house, but... I couldn't go through. I was so scared. I could be stuck there forever!
"Oh no! Argh...!"

Tillie Kett (9)
Bursted Wood Primary School, Bexleyheath

Spy Ninja

Out of nowhere, I woke up to a magical portal. It was a mind-taking one. My eyes bolted open and suddenly, I started getting sucked in...
I ended up in a dark night city with lights shining all over the buildings. Six gangsters appeared and nine policemen. I was on top of a vast tower and I dived off. The bad guys stared up as I was gliding down, but I used my cape to camouflage in the dark sky. I landed on the floor with weapons and nunchucks and took them out quickly.

Jayden Danny Young (9)
Bursted Wood Primary School, Bexleyheath

Craze Game Night

A boy called Jeff found a board game and he got it and went to George. He was surprised! They played it. They opened the game and it sucked them in the game! A wizard said they had to complete the game and to do that, they had to kill the dragon. The boys didn't know what to do! They didn't know the rules, but they didn't care, so they went and played. They got a lot done, but they got killed by the dragon and then they were scared and they never played it again.

Gurinderjit Singh
Bursted Wood Primary School, Bexleyheath

The Lost Soul

There once was a little girl called Mia. She was four years old. One day, her mum let her have a walk in the woods. She loved picking berries and fruit, but then she didn't know how to get back home. She was lost. Then she saw a person in the distance. She stepped a couple of steps forward and then she saw who it was. It was her mum! She ran as fast as she could to hug her mum, then her mum safely walked back home. Mia was so grateful that she had her mum with her.

Neve Barnett (9)

Bursted Wood Primary School, Bexleyheath

Secret Doorway

Once, there was a girl who was twelve years old, her name was Jessica. She went to get a book from her bookcase, then all of a sudden, a trail of mud appeared in a cave. She walked into the ginormous cave and saw lanterns inside with fire in them. She never knew there was a cave inside of her bookcase! After all the walking, she ended up at her front door, then she saw her mum at the front door, and she went in and had dinner. Finally, she went to bed late that night.

Brooke Judy Leutchford (10)
Bursted Wood Primary School, Bexleyheath

Toys Vs Toys

I stepped into the bright portal and woke up as a dragon surrounded by toys. One hit me with a sword and I got up. I roared out to my friends and they came as fast as you could say charge! We charged at the enemy, but they were already ready. It was a tough battle and it had gone on for a while. Dragons fell and the enemy grew small, but we were smaller. After a while, we were starting to win. They struck back at me. We won and we had now taken that part of the land!

Joshua William Kelly (8)
Bursted Wood Primary School, Bexleyheath

The Excellent Mysterious Footballer

As I saw the bright portal, I thought to myself, *do I jump in the portal?* I jumped through the bright portal and found myself on a football pitch. I couldn't believe my eyes; I was playing for the team Arsenal! Aubameyang saw me appear out of nowhere and sprinted across to me. I said to myself, "Why did he sprint to the other side of the pitch?" I was going to cheer him on when suddenly, the portal zapped me up. I was loving my life that day.

Beau (8)
Bursted Wood Primary School, Bexleyheath

The Asteroid

As I saw a sparkle in the sky, I thought it was a shooting star. I charged up to my room and grabbed my telescope. As I put it on my windowsill and looked through the glass, I was petrified. It was a meteor! Could I die this very night, or would I survive?

Suddenly, I saw a different, but smaller, sparkle and my eyes exploded! It was a rocket with missiles, but I noticed it only had one missile, and guess what? It fired its missile and it was bang on target!

Aleks Paul Harrison (11)
Bursted Wood Primary School, Bexleyheath

Rugby Zombie Attacking The Stadium

I woke up and I went in the portal and I saw Twickenham Stadium. There was a dead zombie rugby player and it had a spear. It threw the spear, but I ducked down and quickly grabbed the spear and threw it back at him! Quickly, the zombie dived out of the way. He ran and tackled me to the floor, but I kicked off his head and it went spinning through the air into the goalposts! The zombie died. I had helped the people beat the zombie and saved them with a conversion!

William (8)
Bursted Wood Primary School, Bexleyheath

Midnight!

I woke up in the dark. The whole yellow moon shone bright in the night. I finally came out of my house, wanting to go on the Earth. I flew down and spread my night dust all over the pavement so they knew it was me, Midnight, and that I had come back. I went to every single garden in London and I wouldn't stop. I saw lots of animals on my way, like lions and tigers. I knew my visit was almost at an end, so I flew back to my home and waved goodbye to the Earth.

Misha Madeline Chelsea Clews (9)

Bursted Wood Primary School, Bexleyheath

It's Christmas!

I got out of the portal and the first things I saw were my pointy shoes. I had turned into an elf and I was in Winter Wonderland! One of my elf friends was telling me I had to get to the factory because it was a couple days 'til Christmas, so we had to get to work. I started to make my way to the factory and a snowball came to my face! Luckily, I dodged it.

I finally got to the toy factory. I had a nice greeting. The head sent me to paint the toys.

Evie Stewart-Smith (9)
Bursted Wood Primary School, Bexleyheath

The Unicorn Queen

Once upon a time, there was a unicorn called Rose. She loved to use her powers to make people from the human world happy. One day, Rose was at her palace and she heard a noise downstairs. *Bang!* She was worried that it was her friend. She went downstairs and saw her friend on the floor with blood around her. She saw a knife on the floor. She was confused. She went outside to go to her friend's house to tell her friend's father what happened.

Avneet Kaur Aujla (9)
Bursted Wood Primary School, Bexleyheath

Strong Man

One spooky evening, there was a man called Strong Man. He was a lumberjack. He chopped down a haunted tree, then a ghost came out! Strong Man ran a mile to his house in the middle of the woods, but then the ghost busted down the door! Strong Man ran out and dropped his axe, then ran to a bush and jumped in. While shivering, he looked behind him, then ran to the road, but no one saw the ghost, so he ran to the haunted tree then taped the tree back together.

Ethan Burke (8)
Bursted Wood Primary School, Bexleyheath

The Bottom Of The Ocean For Twelve Hours

I stepped inside the bright portal, then I woke up at the bottom of the ocean. I started swimming for the top of the ocean, but then I felt a hand tug my feet and drag me to the bottom of the ocean. I couldn't breathe. I lost consciousness...
When I woke up, I saw that I had a fin! What was I? Part fish and part girl. I saw five to six girls like me and they took me to a cave.
I woke up the next day and I was happy that I was a human again.

Isobel Puddick (9)
Bursted Wood Primary School, Bexleyheath

Ball World

I stepped into the portal and on the other side there were balls which were people and people were balls. The balls kept kicking all the people and they went flying into the goal. The football people kept on scoring goals. They scored left corner and right corner, then the people went flying into the goal. No one could beat them in football because they could beat you a hundred-nil, so if you tried to win against the footballs, you would lose.

Dylan
Bursted Wood Primary School, Bexleyheath

The Mystery Of The Crown Jewels

On a gloomy day at the Tower of London, the Crown Jewels went missing! It was straight on the news. The king and queen were furious, so they brought in the world-famous detective. He first looked at the fingerprints and he suddenly knew it was TN! The police found him and took the Crown Jewels off him and returned them to the beautiful queen. TN went to prison for fifty years. If you're desperate to know who TN is, he's Thief Ninja.

Mia Rose Vinton (8)

Bursted Wood Primary School, Bexleyheath

Mission Impossible

I was just in a meeting at work when I saw a big purple portal, so I said, "Sorry, sir, I have to go." I went to the wet tree outside and there it was: a portal. It took me to a never-before-seen land, so I went to a big hall and he was there, James Bond, with a lady named Saffron. When I first saw her, I knew that she loved me like I liked her, so after that, I took her back to the modern world. We got married and had babies.

Lenny
Bursted Wood Primary School, Bexleyheath

Life On Osbore!

On a planet named Osbore was a man named Vasian. This planet was tremendously dangerous! Osbore had two sides. One side was 256°C and the side was -325°C.

Vasian was frightened from the shatters on the ground one morning. Suddenly, a huge tsunami happened on the cold side! After thirty minutes and three days, an earthquake happened on the exceedingly hot side. Ponds were shaking like never before, you could even see the lava...

Vasian Soldanescu (9)
Bursted Wood Primary School, Bexleyheath

Murder Most Unpleasant

Deep in the shadows of Sherlock Town was a gate bordering the town. Just on the other side of the gate, it was dull and no person was ever seen there - until now! The National Spy Society had moved their training ground there. They had just solved the mystery of Daisy Gravel. She was caught and slaughtered in the night. It was pitch-black and not one person was in sight...
"Yes, I have finished that level! On to the next!"

Shaan Rai (10)
Bursted Wood Primary School, Bexleyheath

Letter To Harry Potter

Dumbledore was sitting at his oak wood table writing letters to all 11-year-old kids. As he was doing this, the owls were taking the letters. Then an owl went to Daisy's house and dropped it off, then Daisy came and opened the mail. Daisy opened her letter and saw she'd got in to Hogwarts, she was so excited but she didn't realise it was a magic school. Will Daisy be the greatest enchantress? It is a mystery!

Daisy

Bursted Wood Primary School, Bexleyheath

The Bee Attack

As I looked through the bushes in the jungle, I was hunting for meat. I was in there with my brother when I saw an animal. A bee flew right in front of me! I screamed as loud as a lion's roar. I ran back to the tent. I told my brother. He screamed as well! We ran into the jungle mansion and asked my mum to save us. She shut the door behind us. I turned the TV on and thought all about my garden adventure...

Oliver Hill (10)

Bursted Wood Primary School, Bexleyheath

Josh And Joe

Hi, I'm Josh and I'm with Joe! We are explorers and we go back in time to see dinosaurs. We are going sixty million years back in time to see a raptor and to get its claw. There is a woods in front of us and we have heard things in there. It might be a raptor, so when we go in, we have to be careful of what we do. If we make a really loud sound, it might kill us and we won't get its claw...

Joshua R
Bursted Wood Primary School, Bexleyheath

The Assassin

As quick as a cheetah, the man ran. He was running from random people trying to arrest him for a bounty. It was at the dawn of midnight. Ben was dressed in black to blend in with the dark. Ben was trying to get a specific person because he was going to destroy the world. Ben went into the building and used his grappling hook and got up. Suddenly, he jumped up and pushed him down then arrested him.

Sanjeevan Hayer (10)
Bursted Wood Primary School, Bexleyheath

Zooming

As I looked up, I saw the board, all three lights green. It was go time. I started off with a massive *zoom!* The race had begun. I soon started to pick up the pace, then I passed first place and second too. I was first in my red racing car. After a few seconds, I had passed the finish line; I had won! As I got out of the car, I heard my mum say, "Get off the VR!"

Roman Patrick Jameel (10)
Bursted Wood Primary School, Bexleyheath

The Amazing Alpaca-Lypse!

Meowlynx's jaw dropped. Llamas were everywhere! "Mwahaha!" cackled Lady Llamacles. "You'll never stop me, Meowlynx! Just a hundred cats left and I will be your new leader!"

Whilst Lady Llamacles' hysterical laughter echoed across the city, Meowlynx came up with a plan, so she got to work!

After a fifteen-minute-long laugh, Llamacles was puzzled.

"Meowlynx?" she called.

No reply.

She flew around, calling her rival, then...

swoosh! Lady Llamacles got caught in a net!

"Help!" screamed the villain. Meowlynx was about to electrocute her when... *Ring ring!*

Meowlynx woke up. She opened her curtains and gasped...

Reem Abdaal Hakeem (10)
Cherry Orchard Primary School, Birmingham

The Mysterious Rock

The boisterous sounds of the security alarms were blaring wildly across the city centre. Two of the main advanced technology companies had break-ins, but strangely, nothing major was stolen except from some pieces of rocks. Detective Jake, who was investigating the case, found some transparent green sticky substance at the crime scene. The substance was alien when checked by the scientists.

The detective managed to find an alien spaceship. The alien and his ancestors spoke to Jake and told him the reason behind their visit to Earth. Their aim was to save their dying heir to the throne...

Sahil Shubh (9)

Cherry Orchard Primary School, Birmingham

The Figure's Shadow

Droplets of water fell into my hands. The trees danced. As I stepped forward, the trees stooped down, blocking the entrance. I went in. I took a couple more steps and a creepy, mortifying house appeared. Were the lights flickering, or was I blinking too much? My eyes captured a strange, dark figure staring out in one of the windows, getting closer... and closer... and closer. It went from window to window, then the light flickered. Seconds later, the door swung open! As the figure smirked, my spine tingled. Was it fear or dread? I blinked again. 'It' was there...

Reena Kaur Rai (9)
Cherry Orchard Primary School, Birmingham

The Curious Box

Since birth, Tristan had a big imagination and mind. One place that enchanted Tristan was the old abandoned park. To Tristan, each piece of litter was a treasure the most lying on the floor; each patch of long, dry grass was a jungle waiting to happen; each broken swing was a rope to climb Mount Everest!

One day, Tristan was ending his sensational adventure, he found his most remarkable find of all: a curious box. This box was fashioned from dark cherry wood. There were mysterious engravings all over. There were no locks or hinges. This box was special, peculiar...

Ammara Khan (10)
Cherry Orchard Primary School, Birmingham

Case Of The Missing Detective

Lurking on the streets of 5th Avenue was Detective Harlem, looking for his biggest rival yet, J Snicket. As Harlem continued to search the streets, he came to a pause... It was Snicket! Harlem ran as fast as he could to catch him, but Snicket was faster.

Suddenly, Harlem stopped running. He had never seen this part of the city! This could only mean one thing: he was lost and didn't know where to go. Harlem was fuming. Questions like, *where am I?* were running through his mind.

Now, three years later, nobody has a clue where Harlem might be...

Ruqayyah Maryam Sadiq (11)

Cherry Orchard Primary School, Birmingham

Dark Devourer

One night, after sleeping for 259 years, a black, hideous monster called Halmpaf had awoken. The blinding light hurt her five red, glowing eyes, so she quickly made a cloak from blue leaves in the magical forest, then she went out for a midnight stroll.

Just then, she saw something that she hadn't seen before. They were humans! One was called Lily, another was Harry and the rest were Aurora, Jake and Phoebe. They asked Halmpaf questions and then they became superheroes until an evil creature bit Halmpaf and she turned into a crazy beast and ate them all!

Inayah Miah Begum (8)

Cherry Orchard Primary School, Birmingham

Enchanted Forest

Mia stepped into the dark, gloomy portal, wondering where she was going. After she arrived, she was amazed when she saw the mysterious, enchanted forest with rainbow flowers and pure green grass. A beautiful butterfly appeared and Mia went to follow it, but after a while, the butterfly disappeared. By then, Mia was lost deep inside the forest...

After half an hour of walking, Mia came to the edge of the forest and saw rainbow-streaked hair and a golden horn. It had a body as white as snow.

"Wow! This might be the rare, mythical unicorn..."

Maryam Qaadhi (8)
Cherry Orchard Primary School, Birmingham

The Box

A young girl called Stacy didn't like staying home because there was nothing to do. One day, she found a note whilst cleaning the attic. It was a riddle. Carefully, she opened it.

'Congrats on finding this. Now, get ready to go search somewhere underground.'

Stacy knew straight away it was the basement. When she entered, there was a note and a box.

'Well done for finding this.'

Stacy opened the box and saw lots of things that would entertain her. Now she could always check this box whenever she got bored and take it with her everywhere.

Amira Hussain (11)

Cherry Orchard Primary School, Birmingham

My Toy Is Alive And Evil!

There was once a little girl. Before she went missing, she had a teddy called Bobo. When the girl slept, he would awaken. When she was awake, he would fall asleep. She awoke one morning to a trashed bedroom. She assumed it was a robbery, but Bobo knew better. She would wake up with scratches. She thought it was a spider, but Bobo knew better. Jewellery went missing. She assumed it was a theft, but Bobo knew better.

One morning, her mother woke to a missing daughter.

A kidnapping? she thought.

Bobo knew better...

Lilliah Torrens-Pal (11)
Cherry Orchard Primary School, Birmingham

Mysterio

I stood shivering in front of the cupboard in anxiety. I immediately ran downstairs and stayed there for a long time. It took all my courage to go back upstairs. At that moment, the cupboard stopped shaking! With fear, I went to bed and the next morning, my toys had vanished! As I stared in awe at the box, I had to go downstairs. When I went upstairs, my bed had disappeared. Suddenly, a diminutive raven monster sprang up from behind my toy box! This could only mean one thing: monsters still lived! The creature opened its mouth. I fled!

Rishika Bodapati (9)
Cherry Orchard Primary School, Birmingham

The New Prison

One time in a prison, there was a man who got framed in prison. Suddenly, he got bitten by a spider and felt different. He moved his arms and suddenly, the prison got clean! He tried it again. All the prisoners were nice and weren't jerks or bullies. The police were normal and weren't strict. He moved his feet and he could fly!

He went over the fence and escaped. He escaped! He celebrated, but he was just imagining and fainted because of the spider bite...

He got woken up by a policeman who said, "You embarrassed yourself."

Rafan Ali (7)
Cherry Orchard Primary School, Birmingham

The World Of Cubes

I looked around. Where was I? All around me were cubes. There were dark green grass cubes that made up the floor and almost everywhere there were cube trees. I could recognise a few types of trees (birch, oak and spruce), but that didn't matter. All of the clouds were also cubes. I looked at the sun (for some reason, it wasn't hurting my eyes) and predictably, it was a bright, shining square. Then I realised what this was: Minecraft, a game which I thankfully knew a lot about. The problem was, Minecraft had only one way out: death...

Haider Naqvi (10)
Cherry Orchard Primary School, Birmingham

Night Of The Living Lego

I had just had the worst nightmare of my life! It was about my Lego coming to life! As I grabbed my torch to investigate, I saw a Lego monster chewing on my plushie. I tried to shout, but no noise came out. The monster had muted me and had suddenly started to come closer and closer to me. It crawled up my body and started to viciously eat my left ear, then the right and eventually the nose. Finally, it ate everything else...
If you are reading this, unfortunately, it's too late! I have already painfully and silently died...

Piotr Rajkiewicz (9)
Cherry Orchard Primary School, Birmingham

I'm An Angel

There once was a little girl who was as perfect as could be. She was so perfect, in fact, that she was an angel indeed. She had white shoes that shone in the darkness. She had a sparkling white crown, but one day, the crown disappeared! Everyone said, "Go everywhere!"

They searched Asia and then they searched London. In London, there was a boy called Charlie. Charlie said that his dad was a policeman, then he says, "My dad has one robber that could be the robber!"

Then they checked his pockets and he was the robber!

Zoya Yasser (7)
Cherry Orchard Primary School, Birmingham

The Ghost Cabin

One stormy day, a detective was looking for a girl who had been captured. She had been gone for eight months. He was going to look for her. He entered the cabin. It was dark and gloomy, wet and damp - then he heard a noise.

"Oooohhh..."

It was very suspicious... Then he saw five ghosts holding a girl wrapped in rope! He thought in his head, *that must be the girl,* and it was! He chased after the ghosts and he finally caught them. He called the ghost catchers and all the ghosts were put in jail.

Skyler Jeffers-Kelly (9)
Cherry Orchard Primary School, Birmingham

Night Thrasher

On a dark night in Toronto was a man standing in the rain. His name was the Night Thrasher. He was a superhero who defeated a lot of villains.
Two robbers were coming towards him and saying, "Give me your money!" He was never going to let them have his money, so he got his net gun out and shot the net at one of the robbers. He got trapped in there! The other robber was charging at Night Thrasher and Night Thrasher pushed the evil robber and the police came and arrested the robbers. Another win for Night Thrasher!

Jay Karra (8)
Cherry Orchard Primary School, Birmingham

Lost In Space

Once upon a time, there lived an astronaut. She was going to a space mission. She had to save the aliens from the evil monster. Ella the astronaut had just launched her rocket, when suddenly, she started to fall. She luckily had her seatbelt on, but *boom!* She quickly put her helmet on. Ella was fine because a good alien saved her and took her to his planet, Planet Bong. The nice alien gave Ella jelly and Ella defeated the horrible monster. All of the aliens took her to Earth and she lived happily ever after.

Niyah Chohan (8)
Cherry Orchard Primary School, Birmingham

Lizzy's Horrible Dream

Lizzy had a dream and it was a terrifying ordeal. She dreamt that her doll called Simi came to life when she went to sleep.

One day, she woke up at night and noticed that her doll was missing. It had gone downstairs by itself and, to my horror, ate all the food from the fridge and made a mess in the kitchen! The milk was spilt on the floor and Simi's clothes were ruined. I was convinced this was all Simi's fault. I tidied up the mess quickly because my parents would get angry and blame me as always...

Jaspreet Chahal (7)
Cherry Orchard Primary School, Birmingham

A New Life

As I stumbled down a steep hill, I found something unknown. It was not of this world. I decided to take a closer look in curiosity - after all, I am an explorer - but just then, as I raised my head, I found myself in an unknown dimension. It wasn't like Earth - it was filled with ghosts and ghouls which were on the road. Unicorns and aliens flew overhead. I felt like I was in a dream... Wait, I was in a dream! I was stuck there! Was there a way home? I was stuck there all alone!
"Help me!"

Nikhil Dadral (10)
Cherry Orchard Primary School, Birmingham

The New World

There lived a girl called Lilly. She loved exploring, but her mum wouldn't let her. She got grounded but she snuck out from a window. She saw a sign. "I'm going there."
Suddenly, she teleported!
"Wow!" she said with enthusiasm and amazement. "I'm going to explore!"
The world was very big. It had unicorns, pegasuses and talking cotton candy! She had fun in that world. Make sure that you go there and you might see the animals!

Zofia Kieradlo (8)
Cherry Orchard Primary School, Birmingham

The House In The Woods

John opened the creaky door. Silence filled the air. As he stepped in, he listened intently to his footsteps. Smashed bits of glass were littered across the ground, making walking hard. As he slowly tiptoed around the house, he spotted a trail of powder leading into a room. He peeked in. There it was, the ultimate pizza! It had the cheesiest cheese and the juiciest tomato sauce! John held it in awe, took a tremendous bite... then realised it was all a dream!

Amaan Sahonta (11)
Cherry Orchard Primary School, Birmingham

The Spy Hacker

Today I was hacking the system. My name is Ben and I hack and spy. Now, I'm spying on a rich person, so I jump in my Lambo and drive off into the distance. When I get there, I peer through the window and I see a load of money on a table. I got into the air vent and jump down and get £10,000,000 and put it in my bag and run away and get in my car.

When I get back from spying, I park my Lambo and the police come and arrest me for life.

Yusuf Suhail (8)
Cherry Orchard Primary School, Birmingham

I Want To Be One Of Those Girls

I remember when I first started gymnastics, watching the big girls do theirs, and I thought, *I want to be like one of the big strong girls.* So I decided to train every day and come every day. One day, I went to gymnastics and I suddenly had a competition, so I went and luckily, I came first. I was the happiest person ever! Then, every time I went to the gym, I saw little children like I was before, saying, "I want to be like her!"

Marah Ali (7)
Cherry Orchard Primary School, Birmingham

The Stolen Crown

As I snuck into the humongous lab, searching for details about the Queen's stolen crown, I saw a massive PC and on the keyboard was a file saying 'Top Secret: The Queen's Crown'. I opened it and saw all the details I needed to set off and search for the stolen crown.

It's been a long time since then now and I've finally found it in the final location!

Ayaan Salim (8)

Cherry Orchard Primary School, Birmingham

Christmas Catastrophe

It was a few minutes before Christmas Eve when Prickles (Santa's favourite elf) burst into Santa's workshop and cried, "Rudolph's missing!"
For a moment, there was stunned silence, then Tinsel the elderly elf shouted, "Don't be silly! Rudolph's in the sleigh room."
Prickles pleaded, "But he's not, so come and help me search outside!"
As they searched for him, Frost inquired, "Have you checked his favourite field and the barn?"
Prickles answered, "Of course! Mistletoe, go get Santa."
As the elves nervously continued searching, Mistletoe updated Santa.
From deep within the pine trees, Prickles squeaked, "Come quick! I've found something..."

Evelyne Jasmine Rose (9)
Great Hollands Primary School, Bracknell

Disaster Detective

One day, Double Agent Andy was searching for a diamond with his sidekick, Hunter Marbles, when suddenly, he went missing and was never seen again!

Andy put on the secret website: 'Detective Needed!' He instantly got one reply. It was from a lady called Mrs Jones. She got hired within seconds as nobody wanted the job.

She arrived.

"Hello," said Jones quietly.

Andy nodded. He saw the dreadful appearance of her: red lipstick, hair extensions, long nails... Who would wear nails to a detective job?

The first day of the job went horribly as she bragged all about designer clothing!

Molly Jennifer Wise (10)
Great Hollands Primary School, Bracknell

The Unknown Thief

It was Saturday morning and Detective Melia was on a case of theft. Young Sarah had been robbed Friday evening whilst at work at the neighbouring cafe. Witnesses said they heard bangs and crashes at 5:40pm when Sarah had gone midway through her shift. Sarah told Detective Melia she heard noises that she thought were coming from her neighbour's house.

One of the suspects (Bragen Smith) told Melia he was walking his dog around the neighbourhood. Suspect two (Sarah's friend who stayed at her house) said she was cooking and heard noises. Instantly, Detective Melia arrested Sarah's friend - but why?

Anshu Sijapati (10)
Great Hollands Primary School, Bracknell

The Mystical Journey To The Cloud Kingdom

One ordinary day, the teacher told us to stay in our seats while she talked to our headteacher.
Secretly, I snuck up to the board and touched it. Instantly, my body was covered in a rainbow glow! The minute I opened my eyes, there were glittery cotton clouds as a floor and there was a special sparkle. OMG! There were unicorns! There was a big one speaking, saying, "Our cloud kingdom is in danger - please help!"
Just then, a ferocious roar shattered the sky. Dragons, big, grim sky dragons, nested on the unicorns' rainbows. One spat flames! Argh!

Madison Atkinson (11)
Great Hollands Primary School, Bracknell

The Tale Of Abbie Swan, The Stolen Child

Many years ago, a young girl named Abbie was kidnapped in the woods while wandering back home. The trees were swaying viciously in the breeze and the grass tied together, knotting the soggy ground...

Good morning everyone! This is about me, Abbie Swan. I am enjoying my life now, if you count being sucked through a magical portal as an option. 'How did I do this?' people may ask. Well, one bitter evening when the frost was crisping up, I knew it was time to leave the cellar I was trapped in. I ran away and spotted a mysterious flower...

Erin Olivia Tobin (11)
Great Hollands Primary School, Bracknell

The Mystic Land Unicorns Are Real!

Once, there was a little girl. Her friend Amber and her were assigned to go to Mystic Land. Sapphire and Amber gasped!
"Mrs Accaraley will give us such a hard thing to do!"
Sapphire spent all last night developing a chemical. We trembled before the waterfall of magic. I fell into the waterfall! I ran out and saw unicorns! I ran after them. There were two of them. I used the chemical and me and Amber were in the sky. We were half-unicorn! We thought, *oh no!* We went to school and everyone wanted to play with us!

Lily-Mae Goode (8)
Great Hollands Primary School, Bracknell

A Giant In The World!

Once upon a time, there was a superhero in the world. She was there because she solved crimes there. One time, there was a stinkbomb created by a giant!

However, this time, the giant came down himself and people tried to defeat him. All the giant ate was trees (which he thought were broccoli). The superhero had an idea! If the giant ate the trees, he would go back!

They let the giant eat. When the giant saw there were no more trees, he went back where he came from. Everybody was excited, then they had a party!

Ynette Ng Hill (7)
Great Hollands Primary School, Bracknell

The Dark Exploration

One dark night, an explorer was looking in the forest. He found a hut, just made. Had he looked there before? Maybe not. Was it a dream?
As he looked behind him, a dark shadow was hovering above him. He ran, but he wasn't going anywhere. Claws slashed his face! He was asking himself, "Why me?"
He ran away at last. He woke up in his bed. Was it a dream? He looked in his mirror. The scratch marks were still there. How did he end up in his bed? He touched his scratch mark. It was still bleeding...

Art Stevens (10)
Great Hollands Primary School, Bracknell

Secrets

I have a secret. Can I tell you? Everyone has secrets but I've never told mine. My secret isn't horrible or scary, but people wouldn't accept me if they knew it. I love my secret, but it can be lonely not being able to tell anyone. I have lots of friends, but none of them suspect I am hiding this from them. It's hard keeping my secret. Nobody knows the true me.

The time has come to share my secret. I am nervous about sharing my secret. I worry I will be rejected... But I have made my decision...

Isabella Florence Rose (8)
Great Hollands Primary School, Bracknell

The Doll In The Haunted House

The dirty vagabond was only twenty-five years old. The cold rain soaked him and he shivered. Luckily, he saw an abandoned, derelict house high on a cliff overlooking the damp beach. As he entered the house, he saw the staircase was broken, so he lay down on the floor, exhausted. He noticed an ugly doll sitting on the fireplace before he went to sleep. He woke with a start with the doll jumping on him and he ran out of the house screaming as loud as he could. He was so afraid and shaking that he never returned again.

Mollie Patrice Waterton (8)

Great Hollands Primary School, Bracknell

The Myth About Unihedge

Once upon a time, there was a myth about a unihedge. A unihedge is a mix between a unicorn and a hedgehog. Obviously, I made it up.
So, there was a unihedge and let's say it was very mischievous. It got up to all kinds of things you may not know, like, he used to sneak around your house, rummaging for food. He also used to steal things from you like shoes and a bunch of other things. The unihedge was called Dark Moon. He was also very robotic and evil. He did not like people making fun of him...

Jessica Amy Royle (10)
Great Hollands Primary School, Bracknell

The Story Of Two Detectives And A Thief

It all started with two people who were detectives and a thief who was trying to steal a document. He always got caught every time by the detectives, but this time, the thief had a much better plan, which was to make a device to become invisible so the detectives could not see him and he could steal the document without them stopping him. The detectives couldn't stop the thief from stealing the top-secret document and he got it back to his master! Would he destroy the detectives once and for all...?

Jamie Barnard Berry (10)
Great Hollands Primary School, Bracknell

Space Wars

On Sunday, Roy leapt out of bed and ran to the basement. He got his dad's shovel and was digging. His metal detector spotted something. He hit something. He pressed a button and this big vortex sucked him up and took him into a UFO! He was surrounded by aliens holding laser swords. They gave him one and took him to a black hole for a fight! Roy was nervous. There were monsters. One ran up to Roy, but he sliced it in half. It was over and Roy went to the vortex, proud.

Xavi Khan-Sharma (10)
Great Hollands Primary School, Bracknell

The Disappearing!

Once, there lived a girl called Emma who was courteous. She was a budding detective! One day, she heard the news about the disappearance of a precious pearl from a renowned museum. She set out that night, found some handprints and scanned them.

Following day, she attended a luxurious ceremony. Emma acted quickly and darted towards the security. Whenever someone came in or came out, Emma would scan their hand. Eventually, the thief was found due to her diligent effort. Emma reported it to the police and the thief was jailed. The pearl was returned back safely to the museum.

Umathapasvi Kakarlapudi (9)

Hounslow Heath Junior School, Hounslow

Journey Of The Mountain Climber

Once, there were three people climbing up to the mountains.

"The mountain is thousands of miles in length, I suppose," said Bob.

They climbed and camped there for ten days (seven days climbing and three days rest). They thought, *it is going to take ages.*

Finally, they reached the top and rested there for one day. The next day, they went outside, but Kevin was missing, so they started to find him. How could they find Kevin?

Suddenly, Stuart saw Kevin's gloves on the floor! They found him hanging on the mountain, trying to reach to the top...

Parag Mittal (10)

Hounslow Heath Junior School, Hounslow

The Future Portal

I panted, out of breath, as I hauled myself up the countless rocks and boulders. The view of the summit emerged into sight and, finally, I hitched myself, sweating and exhausted, onto the great mountain which overlooked the forest. Sinking onto a large flat boulder, I spotted a diminutive little box. I reached out, grabbed it and prised open the miniature lid. Inside was a mass of airy substance which, when touched, sucked my body into it!

I landed in a city with air-trains, video games on people's hands, but no plants - none at all! This was the future...

Shraddha Kori (9)
Hounslow Heath Junior School, Hounslow

The Mysterious Creature

Once, there was a little adventurous girl who loved animals. She went to the eerie and misty forest. Suddenly, Lilly realised that she was lost. After a while, she came across the silent, screaming mouth of a cave where she discovered a ferocious creature with enormous wings trapped in a net. She got a little bit frightened, but she helped the scary-looking creature by cutting through the net with a sharp-edged stone. The creature was grateful and relieved and showed Lilly her way back home. As a result, both Lilly and the creature became very good friends forever.

Harim Khan (11)
Hounslow Heath Junior School, Hounslow

The Room

There was a girl called Anika. One day, it was her eleventh birthday. After the cake was cut, the door opened all by itself, then she walked in.

All of a sudden, the door shut, then a man appeared out of nowhere! The man said, "This will help you find the key in the teacup..."

The clue said: 'Find the key at the end of the teacup.'

Anika looked everywhere until she found a teacup. She smashed it. She found the key. She tried every door, but nothing worked!

Then the key said, "Unleash your power!"

She went home.

Khushi Puni (10)

Hounslow Heath Junior School, Hounslow

The Underground World

There was a spoilt boy called Zayan who lived in a magnificent mansion. His parents were ridiculously rich and always bought whatever he wanted.
One day, Zayan discovered a door under his big bed as big as an elephant! He could be mischievous at times, and so he went down. As soon as he did, he found himself on a roller coaster which buckled Zayan itself and off it went! He screamed! This was a rocking roller coaster!
Finally, the ride ended, but he realised he was in an underground world!
"Oh no!" he sighed. What would he do now?

Eshal Waqas (9)
Hounslow Heath Junior School, Hounslow

A White Christmas In Spain

Mika and Mike were in bed wishing that this year it would snow - but they lived in Madrid...

The next morning, they did something bizarre: they mailed themselves to the North Pole! It took hours and hours to get there, but once they arrived, they were amazed! There was snow everywhere! They dashed past heaps of trees and elves until they found a door which said *Snow Room*. Mika kicked the door open to see a big digital map. Mike tapped Spain and pressed a big red button. Hooray! They did it! Spain finally had a white Christmas!

Prisha Kapoor (9)

Hounslow Heath Junior School, Hounslow

The Strong Friendship

Once upon a time, a monkey was playing flute to his friends on his favourite tree. Suddenly, with a strange noise, a creepy man appeared from a dark cave. He spotted the monkey's favourite tree to make his boat from. All the animals were frightened and all hid behind the bushes. As the man started chopping the tree, the monkey and his friends were so sad that they made up a plan to attack the man, and *swoosh!* They went swinging, jumping, hitting and kicking, and soon the man was defeated and all of the animals lived happily ever after.

Simionie Galami (10)
Hounslow Heath Junior School, Hounslow

Heaven Or Hell?

I raced across the streets and I was bleeding. I stopped dead, hearing the sound of laughter. A kitten crawled into a bush and was devoured almost instantly! Anxiously, I followed the kitten. At that moment, I was no longer at a dead end! It was cold and snowing.

Suddenly, a girl screamed at me, "Get inside, the ghosts are going to kill you!"

I laughed at her like she was crazy. Without a warning, something clawed at my ankle! Was she right that ghosts existed here? Would I go to Heaven or Hell? Or was I already in Hell...?

Rishika Balaji (9)
Hounslow Heath Junior School, Hounslow

The Lost Creature

Me and my brother Jimmy were always the adventurous type, so when we heard rumours of the new species, zybog, we were flabbergasted and straight away got to the case. People had always said they'd seen it somewhere near in the Atlantic Ocean.

One day, we decided to set off with our heads held high. When we finally reached our destination. We dived in and saw the world of water. Suddenly, we had found the creature. It seemed lost, so we tried to direct it to its parents. When we did, it looked relaxed and lived happily with its family.

Rihab Belbahi (10)
Hounslow Heath Junior School, Hounslow

The Amazon Saver

On the street of Lanel was a girl called Mandy.
Once a week, Mandy checked the news. One day,
Mandy went on the news and saw the Amazon
rainforest was in danger. Mandy freaked out! She
asked her mom to give her a journey. Mum said no,
so Mandy snuck out of the house...
Six months later, Mandy saw hot, flaming fire in
her eyes. Mandy got her equipment and turn by
turn, step by step, she carefully saved our planet!
Ten years later, Mandy was the most famous
person because of saving our planet and being a
courageous saviour.

Denis Popescu (10)
Hounslow Heath Junior School, Hounslow

The Mysterious Visit To Grandma's House

There was a girl called Maddy who had a younger brother, Max. Their mum was working and they stayed at their grandma's, but this visit was strange. The dog didn't bark at all, Lily didn't play, and worst, whilst they drew, there was a passage and a secret door! They followed it and there was a creepy witch! They screamed, ran back to their grandma and called the police and their mum immediately.

A few days later, they found out that she was a very bad lady and she had been wanted for a while...

Zahraa Khan (10)

Hounslow Heath Junior School, Hounslow

Blooming Joy

As the sun rose, children woke smiling, but for Fay, it was gloomy again. This day, little Fay found a way in middle May to find the joy all girls and boys needed to smile all day. To find that joy was easy; all she needed to do was open her mind and recall all those good times with joy, so the joy went up inside and bloomed like fresh flowers. She spread the smile she had on her face from person to person, place to place. The magical smile spread like wildflowers blooming in a lovely green field.

Melissa Rodrigues (11)
Hounslow Heath Junior School, Hounslow

The Secret Door

Hi, my name is Daisy and my life sucked 'til something changed that. I went to the jungle! It was amazing! But I soon got tired and relaxed on a huge rock. It was annoying! I hurt my back, but decided to check what was happening, so I turned around and found a door, so I opened it and went inside bravely. There was a bit of light, but as I went on, it turned darker and darker. I could barely see anything! I just kept going ahead, more and more nervous, 'til I saw it...

Shokria Yaqubi (11)
Hounslow Heath Junior School, Hounslow

Space Mission

Five, four, three, two, one, blast off! The rocket Apollo 11 with me, astronaut Ken, blasted away into outer space. I looked out the round window, then I saw a big planet. It was Jupiter! Then I saw a purple planet. It was the scary alien planet! I landed on it. I saw a green alien! I wasn't scared because he was smiling at me.
"Hi, where're you from?"
"I'm from the blue planet. We call It Earth."
I went back to the space rocket and I sent an email to the base: 'Mission completed. We're not alone in space.'

Antoni Lenczowski (7)
Kennoway Primary School, Kennoway

Space Adventure

The rocket blasted off to Planet Mars. When we landed on Planet Mars, we found some space friends that were actually aliens. I couldn't understand them and I had to go back home to Planet Earth soon, but before I went home, I played with the cool aliens. Then I tried to catch shooting stars and I started to know some alien language. Finally, I had to go back home to Planet Earth and I told my friends and family about all my amazing and funny adventures in outer space!
I can't wait for my next adventure!

Lexi Anderson (7)
Kennoway Primary School, Kennoway

Space Adventure

Bob and family went to a space station and you could actually go to the moon, so he said, "I want to go to the moon."

He suited up, then said bye. Bob was excited to go on his space adventure to the amazing moon and planets.

"Yes!" he called. "Five, four, three, two, one, blast off!"

Then, after a while, he got hungry, so he ate his sandwich then landed on Planet Mars! Finally, he got into his suit and got his Mars Buggy 20000 and drove around Mars to find alien life...

Daniel McGonagle (7)

Kennoway Primary School, Kennoway

Space Adventure

Three, two, one, zoom! The rocket went off into the galaxy and the planets were spectacular, so astronauts Harley and Lexi went to explore them. First, they went to Planet Neptune. It was the coldest planet. They danced on it and then they saw a very strange alien. They asked the alien if it wanted to dance and it did! It was fun dancing together, but then they both noticed a shiny sparkle from the ground. They picked it up and it was a shiny, rare space rock! They all danced with enjoyment and took it back home.

Harley McVey (7)
Kennoway Primary School, Kennoway

Space Mission

Suddenly, the rocket went *woosh* into outer space and I bumped into a big alien! It said, "Hello, my name is Bob!"

"My name is Astronaut Lucas. I have a little brother. He is annoying, so I didn't bring him on the mission."

I had to explore Planet Venus to find rocks that were special to save Planet Earth. On my mission, I saw lots of interesting aliens. One said, "Hello, my name is Jay. I come from a planet far, far away. Can you take me back to Earth?"

Lucas Jackson Innes (7)
Kennoway Primary School, Kennoway

Space Adventure

I went to outer space to find Planet Venus, but suddenly, the rocket crashed! *Bang! Crash!* Then I saw an alien! It was weird, but then it pushed me onto a scary planet...

I didn't know the scary planet. It was cold. I saw a massive rocket, so I said, "Help! I am alone on this planet! The aliens are going to get me!"

There was no answer from the massive rocket, so I started to plan my great escape mission back to Planet Earth...

Freya Anderson (7)
Kennoway Primary School, Kennoway

Space Mission

Once, there lived a man called Kelven and he was going to Jupiter in a space rocket. One, two, three, blast off! He went fast into outer space!
He arrived at Jupiter and he met an alien. He kept on rubbing his eyes. He kept on rubbing and rubbing and the alien said, "Hello there!"
The man went back into the rocket and got his super-fast moon buggy and his camera and he took photos, then went back to Earth and showed all his pictures to everyone.

Lewis McGonagle (7)
Kennoway Primary School, Kennoway

Space Mission

I, Alien Robot, went to space. My mission was to get a bit of water from Mars. I landed on Mars. On Mars, I built a base. There were lots of soy aliens. One spilt some Mars water. I took it to my base. I built a space buggy. I put a bit of the Mars water in the buggy. I needed a sticker of an alien to activate the buggy because the fuel ran out. I managed to find it and got the buggy working. Finally, I could go home happy. The mission was completed!

Filip Mis (7)
Kennoway Primary School, Kennoway

Space Adventure

Astronaut McIlroy got in his suit. He went in his massive rocket. Blast off! He went in his rocket and landed on Planet Jupiter. It was very hot! He wore a sunsuit and then he went in his buggy to explore Planet Jupiter. He was wandering around for some space rocks. Some were shiny and some were plain white.

He got back in his buggy and bumped into a sparkly alien! It was a very friendly alien. He gave the alien a lift in his cool space buggy.

Jimi McIlroy (7)
Kennoway Primary School, Kennoway

Space Mission

Hi, my name is Kaysen. Before I got on the rocket, I needed to make sure that I had all of my space stuff to go on my space mission. Next, I blasted off to the moon. The moon was so cool and bright! I found moon rocks - it was very fun.

Suddenly, there was an alien, but it was a friendly alien. His name was Calum and we started to be friends. Then there were more aliens, but they were bad! We ran into the rocket and zoomed away to outer space!

Kaysen Robertson (7)

Kennoway Primary School, Kennoway

Space Adventure

My dad and I went to the space centre to get the biggest rocket ready to fly to space. It would take four days to get there.

When we got to Planet Mars, our mission was to find giant gems to bring home for gifts. We all saw video aliens that were rare.

When it was time to go home, I gave the aliens some space cookies which floated in space and they were very rare to catch. We then went home to Earth with the gems.

Riley Wilson (7)
Kennoway Primary School, Kennoway

Space Mission

At lightning speed, astronaut Kaiden put on his spacesuit, then got into his rocket. One, two, three, blast off! He went to the moon on his mission to find alien life.

When he got to the moon, he explored, then heard a noise. It sounded like an alien. It was twenty aliens! He was shocked! He was so happy! He played for about three hours, then he had to go. He said, "Goodbye!" then zoomed back to Earth.

Cooper McKinstray (7)
Kennoway Primary School, Kennoway

Space Adventure

One day, an extremely long rocket took off into space. It zoomed into space, passing Planet Mars, then went back to the moon to collect moon rocks. Suddenly, they heard a mysterious voice saying, "Astronaut Mary and Astronaut Romy, how are you?"
They got a big fright because an alien jumped out of a space bush!
The alien said, "Don't be scared, I won't hurt you."

Marli Auchterlonie (7)
Kennoway Primary School, Kennoway

Space Adventure

I went to space in Apollo 11, the rocket. I landed on the moon. When I went on the moon, I said, "Oh, how are you?"

I was amazed - it was an alien! The alien was called Max. At first, I was scared of alien Max because he had red googly eyes.

I built a space shuttle as quickly as I could. The alien got his ship and kept shooting my space shuttle. It was scary, but I managed to escape to safety!

Leo Davis (7)

Kennoway Primary School, Kennoway

Space Mission

There were only two people that were brave enough to go to space: Lexi and Tulisa. They had to explore lots of planets. It was amazing!
On Planet Venus, they saw a tiny pink alien called Sprinkles. Tulisa and Lexi and Sprinkles made friends. They played on the moon. It was fun! They found a rainbow rock!
It was time to go back to Earth and they brought Sprinkles back to Planet Earth!

Tulisa McBride
Kennoway Primary School, Kennoway

Space Adventure

One, two, three, blast off! Apollo 15 went to Planet Mars to explore! Mars was very hot. Mars was orange. Astronaut Macii went searching to find some aliens, but then she found a space rock right in front of her! It was amazing! She loved exploring the galaxy and she took her beautiful space rock home to show her family. They were amazed with her incredible space rock!

Macii Fyfe (7)
Kennoway Primary School, Kennoway

Space Mission

I got on my giant rocket and I went to Mars on an adventure. I saw a friendly alien who had twenty eyes and orange, bumpy skin. I was the first person to touch Planet Mars. It felt very hot and bumpy! I took some rocks so I could give them to my astronaut boss back on Planet Earth.

Evan Alistair Michael Cation (7)
Kennoway Primary School, Kennoway

Space Mission

Three... two... one... blast off! The rocket zoomed up into space with Astronaut Tom. He wanted to explore Planet Jupiter. He found an extremely rare alien called Gold. Tom and Gold went for tea. They had pizza, then Tom went back to Earth and he brought alien Gold with him.

Kiko (7)
Kennoway Primary School, Kennoway

Space Adventure

Before I could go to space, I had to put five boosters on my space rocket so I could go super fast into space. Then I landed on Venus. It was hot and I saw an alien turtle. It was happy! She waved to me, then we ate yummy space doughnuts and big alien cookies.

Alishba Rehman (7)

Kennoway Primary School, Kennoway

Space Adventure

I went to space with an astronaut, Rex, in a space rocket to find aliens. When we were going to space, Rex crashed into the large moon! We fixed the amazing rocket. I got out the space toolbox to fix the space rocket so Rex and I could go back home.

Jay Pile (7)
Kennoway Primary School, Kennoway

The Truth Of Area 51

Three boys called Billy, Taylor and William all dreamed of exploring Area 51, so they did!

"Wow, so that's the gate," said Billy.

"Please, I don't want to go. Look, it says 'Stop!'," whined William.

"Lets go!" Taylor said excitedly.

They went in and, almost immediately, a bunch of armoured cars met them.

"Oh no!" exclaimed Billy.

"Put your hands up!" boomed an officer.

They all ran as quickly as they could and suddenly bumped into a green creature.

They all gasped,

"Alien!" they screamed and ran back out.

"Get in the car!"

And off they went into the distance...

Billy Albone (8)
Potton Lower School, Potton

Death Of The Zigoo Monster

It was a cold day and Agent Virus was shooting pheasants. He was a villainous spy who was trying to solve a hard mystery because the power source was drained. Agent Virus was a friend of nobody and lived in the Laser Pit in Shadow Alley. His arch-nemesis was the Zigoo Monster, a poison-spitting monster that could possess people. He was the suspect for the mystery and, just then, a huge thing ran into Shadow Alley and said, "Let our battle begin!"

Virus shot the beast numerous times. Zigoo fell because of the lasers, but then Virus died...

Alfie Navi (9)
Potton Lower School, Potton

The Battle Of Britain

One grizzly, grey afternoon, I was sitting in a muddy ditch with all the other British soldiers. The Germans were in the ditch opposite us. Although we were meant to be battling, we were going to have our football final today.

I suddenly heard a German voice shouting, "Are you going to come play?"

So all the British sprinted up the ladder to play the game.

One long hour later, the ref signalled there was one minute left. Five... four... three... two... goal! The British players were taking their shirts off! England had just won one-nil!

Noah Wright (9)

Potton Lower School, Potton

The Criminal Mermaid!

Once, there was a young princess mermaid who was trying to take over the world - but first, she had to win the battle. Her eyes couldn't stop blinking when she saw the other team!

"We need to be twice as hard to win this battle!"

She practised every day. You could really tell that, every day, she wanted this. Sweat dripped off her tail. As she was in bed, she wondered if she would win or not.

When it came to that day, they got ready, but then thought, *it's not about winning, just trying.* They won. Yippee!

Isla Maney (9)
Potton Lower School, Potton

Under The Bed

Tom sat on his bed, thinking about all the space planets. He stepped off his bed. Suddenly, something grabbed him by the leg and pulled him under the bed! He fell for ages, then he hit the ground with a thump. He was on Jupiter, but he was stuck in a bunker. He bellowed for help. Just then, a little green head poked out from the corner.

"Hi! My name is Jeff," he said. "Do you need help?" He led him through his tunnels to a rocket. They got in. The engine started. They set off! Suddenly, the engine failed...

Taylor Anthony Hutchison (9)
Potton Lower School, Potton

The Alien Bank Robber

Dave got into his rocket and went into space, but then he heard a random sound: *meep! Meep, meep, meep!*
Where did that come from? he thought. He saw a big greeny-yellow structure. It was an alien bank! The meep was from an alien saying, "Go away!" It was trying to protect the alien bank!
Soon, Dave had set up a trap to get rid of the alien. He made a portal to a nearby black hole and it worked perfectly! Next, he looked inside the bank and lots of green and yellow money stared back at him...

Samuel Hill (8)
Potton Lower School, Potton

Visitor On Prehistoric Earth

One day, an alien called Flesh Eating Jiont came. Eighty million years ago, he crashed. He saw a crocodile jumping out of the water and eating a velociraptor! He hid. He got chased by a tyrannosaurus rex! He ran away as fast as he could.

It was night-time. He went to sleep and, the next morning, he built a house and made a sword and shield and killed a velociraptor. He found coal and made a fire.

Something was shaking! He hid and he thought he was going to die, but it was his ship and he went back home.

Joshua Dennis Daniel Oswald (8)
Potton Lower School, Potton

Dog Zombie Mayhem

There was once a young boy called Burt. He was really into history. One day, he built a time machine, but it didn't work. He kept on trying to make his masterpiece. Finally, one time, it worked! It was the coolest thing he had ever made.

He wanted to travel back in time. Suddenly, he had an idea. If he went now, he could make it back for dinner, so he got into the time machine. One minute later, he made it to his destination. The place was filled with dog zombies! Would he survive this disaster...?

Angelo Cucchiara (9)
Potton Lower School, Potton

Earth Saver

I am Agent Boble and I am on my way to my spaceship because a killer meteor is heading for Earth! If I do not stop it, all Earthlings will die! Twenty minutes have passed. I have the meteor in sight. As I zoom up to it, it destroys my ship!
I have stopped the meteor, but now I'm stranded! How long will this go on for...?
A hundred years later, I'm still in space... Now I see a black hole! As I am quickly sucked in, I know my time is up. Goodbye...!

Florence Isabelle Whittaker (9)

Potton Lower School, Potton

Ghost World

I heard a scream! It was coming from the haunted house, the house no one dared to enter. The last time someone went in, they never came back, but I decided to go in anyway. I picked the lock on the door, went in - then it all went black. The lights turned off by themselves. It was like there was a ghost... and there was a ghost - no, a hundred ghosts. The place was full of them!
I found a gun full of slime. I shot the ghosts with it. They disappeared - for now...

Florence Thomas (9)
Potton Lower School, Potton

The Mythical Adventure

I'd just stopped outside the door of my cabin and saw the most beautiful sight of my life: a unicorn. Jeffry came. I called him my sidekick.

"Woof!" he said.

We set off with our bags.

"Look, it's Santa and he's on a unicorn!" I just loved unicorns and Santa. Jeffry didn't know what a unicorn or Santa was, but he was excited anyway. Suddenly, we found out we were lost, so they took us back home.

Bella Aghera (9)
Potton Lower School, Potton

Trick Or Treat Disaster!

Logan had been waiting for this moment forever. He was just going to go trick or treating as an alien. First, he went up to Mrs Trickle's door and shouted, "Trick or treat!" She gave him a treat. Next, he went up to his new neighbour's house. He bellowed, "Trick or treat!" again, but this time, a man shoved something in his mouth and closed the door. He swallowed it. He was just about to walk away, but he fainted!

Bethany Kindon (9)
Potton Lower School, Potton

Is It True?

Once, there was a mermaid. She wanted to rule the abyss. She was evil. She had done many criminal things. She was quite like Ursula if you ask me! She had no heart or friends. She swam to her castle and planned her evil kill so she could steal the crown.

"You don't know who you are dealing with!" she shouted. She got her cauldron and cast the most evil spell ever. One by one, they all disappeared...

Alannah Judd (9)
Potton Lower School, Potton

One Day In Wonderland

"Go on then, roll the dice!"

Tallie and her friends, Belle and Briar, were playing her new game. Tallie rolled the dice, but she didn't get a chance to see what she'd rolled as a small green portal appeared in front of them. Tallie touched it and she, Belle, Briar and Bea the dog, who was watching them, fell in. They were all speechless as a wonderland appeared!

"You're here!" said a small rabbit.

"We're where?" asked Tallie.

"I am the White Rabbit," he said. "Someone is plotting to kill Wonderland's queen. I need your help! Time is running out..."

Tilly Gorgeous Leah Swift (10)

St Peter's Primary Academy, Easton

Break Time

Rio, Lilly and Miles were playing outside in the cold, breezy, uninspiring playground.

"It!" Miles cried, touching Lily's soft blue arm. Lily charged after Rio. Rio was running away when Lily pushed him. Rio fell to the floor with a thud. Rio had hit his head and now there was blood everywhere. Rio was lying on the hard floor unconscious...

Rio was in his first lesson at his new school. They were shouting their powers to each other. It was Rio's go. Rio started hovering, then he started flying! Then, almost suddenly, their teacher shouted, "Break!"

Then Rio woke up...

Eleanor Crocker (10)

St Peter's Primary Academy, Easton

Galaxy Hole

This is a girl named Lily's story. One day, Lily went in her kitchen, but when she got in, something was wrong: there was a big black hole!

"Argh!" shrieked Lily. "I think I need to investigate in there." She then exclaimed, "I am going in!"

She then dashed into the black hole. When she got in, she was located in a galaxy. It had purples, blues and pinks splattered everywhere. It was extraordinary! She was also hovering in mid-air. She felt like a ballerina dancing Swan Lake. But finally, after all this fun, something tugged her leg...

Livia Trett (10)

St Peter's Primary Academy, Easton

The Shockwave Mystery

On a stormy night, FBI Agent Lewis arrived at the high-tech weapon laboratory. The deadly shockwave gun had been stolen. Lewis uncovered a piece of the thief's ripped clothing. He tested it using his scanning machine and got a positive ID. He jumped in his car and roared up to a disused factory. At the boarded-up door, he shouted, "FBI! Open up!"

No response. He kicked the door down and spotted a mysterious figure running. Lewis pulled him to the floor and cuffed him. It was none other than his FBI pal Ellis!

"Mission completed!" Lewis cheered with excitement.

Jake Lewis Betts (10)

St Peter's Primary Academy, Easton

The Disappearance Of King Alfredo

King Alfredo was resting on his golden throne at the end of a long table of food, waiting for everyone to come for breakfast. When everyone came for breakfast, King Alfredo was not there! Queen Adelane sent out the knights to try and find the king, but they could not find him...

The next day, near the king's throne, they noticed some muddy footprints leading out of the castle. They followed the footprints and they led to the Black Knight's castle. It must have been the Black Knight! They went in and found the king in a dusty cellar.

"Hooray!"

Jacob Wilde (10)
St Peter's Primary Academy, Easton

The Aliens

Once, there was a girl called Rosie. She was home alone, chilling on the sofa. Suddenly, she heard a knock on the door. It looked like an alien! He grabbed her and flew away...

When she got to the alien and ghost land, she looked at her arm. She could hardly see it! She looked in a window. They're aliens on roller skates! She went down a road and went into her house. Her mum was calling her name. Rosie said, "I'm here!" but her mum couldn't hear her, then an alien came and took her!

Her mum said, "Help!"

Summer-Jade Bevis (9)

St Peter's Primary Academy, Easton

The Killer Clown

Once, there were two girls called Rose and Bella. They went on holiday to a campsite. It was night-time and they heard a noise outside of the tent. Bella saw a torch in their tent and grabbed the torch, but Bella accidentally dropped the torch. Rose leant over and grabbed the torch, but suddenly, a killer clown grabbed Rose and disappeared with her! Rose was terrified...
Bella was scared because she was on her own, but then Bella saw another killer clown running towards her! Suddenly, they both heard each other scream really loud...

Olivia Stangroom (10)
St Peter's Primary Academy, Easton

Away With The Wind

I step into a vast, gloomy screen. I'm transported onto a cloud, heading towards my house at lightspeed. I suddenly realise I've travelled back in time! The house is much smaller, so obviously I wasn't born - but wait... Where's Dad? Mum says Dad always got home early.

Anyway, how did I become a ghost? Oh, who cares. Let's check out my house while it's possible!

Wait... There is an axe, and there is Dad's dead body! Now I know why Mum never talks about Dad: she murdered him! I can't live with this, so I'll follow the wind...

Isabella Shaw (10)

St Peter's Primary Academy, Easton

Suspicious Hallows Eve!

There was once a girl and she was all alone, but then a ghost appeared! The creepy ghost said, "You must read this scroll that I give you or something horrible will happen to you."
When the ghost had said that, the girl remembered what her mum had told her: never trust or talk to strangers or take what they give to you. But then she thought, *I don't want something horrible to happen to me!* So she opened it even though she didn't want to. She couldn't believe what it said...

Imogen Easton (9)
St Peter's Primary Academy, Easton

The Missing Ballet Shoes

My name is Piper and I love ballet. I have my lessons on Saturdays, so I pack my ballet bag on Friday nights and leave it in the hall.

One morning, I zipped my bag shut and off we went. When I began to change, I discovered that my shoes were missing, so we had to go home to get them. I ran up to my room to fetch them, but couldn't find them. My mum shouted, "I've found them!"

I ran downstairs and there was my puppy with my shoes. The little scamp had taken them from my bag!

Eleanor Elsie Miller (9)
St Peter's Primary Academy, Easton

The Doll Is Haunting Me!

As I stepped into my room, I suddenly felt a shiver down my spine. I turned around in horror but saw nothing. I turned back in disbelief and there it was, a doll, one creepier than the creepiest circus clown you've ever seen! As I stared at it, I attempted to move, but I couldn't move an inch. Suddenly, my legs started to move towards the doll. In my head, I heard laughing from the doll and I started to laugh hysterically. I tried to stop, but I fainted, and when I woke up... I was the doll!

Imogen Rose Jarvis (9)
St Peter's Primary Academy, Easton

The Stolen Mona Lisa

One day, the Mona Lisa was stolen and Alex was ready to save the world - but would he go? Alex was part of a secret agent team called S11MOSO. Only two agents would go and they were Jeano and... Alex!
They set off in an avocado-green jet. On the way, Jeano disappeared and Alex was alone. He went to France to find it and found a base that was big and dark. He walked in and there it was! He distracted the thief by making noises and, as slimy as a snake, he took it...

Safal Neupane (10)

St Peter's Primary Academy, Easton

Weird Things

One day, there was a boy who went missing in the woods. Police came, and a murder mystery person called David. He was a set piece specialist. He looked at the child and said he was killed by a demon alien, so the police went on a hunt for a UFO. They found a UFO, so they searched it and found a dead demon. It was creeping them out badly!

Harry James Mills (9)
St Peter's Primary Academy, Easton

The Day Peculiar People Arrived

Today on a boat, some peculiar white men arrived. They told us a story about a yellow rock called gold.

After that, I said, "Hi, my name is Gloom Thunder. I am Native America."

"I am Zoe."

Then Zoe told me about the Mayflower and we made a fire. It was fun! Goodnight!

Taylor Osborne (9)
St Peter's Primary Academy, Easton

Loki And Odin Have A Fight

"Bad weather is better than good weather," muttered Odin. "It gives us water for life!"

"No, no, no!" commented Loki. "Sun will make people happy and flowers will grow!"

"Guys," said Thor, "stop arguing! We need all the elements for the world to be beautiful. Stop arguing and work together, please."

"Okay," pronounced Odin and Loki.

"Let's work together," said Odin.

"Okay then, shall we go to the woods? Let's go and kill some animals for everyone's dinner."

They had pigs, sheep and cows and a nice, big, huge horse! They all fell asleep, but they heard something...

Emily Deakin-Jones (8)

St Wystan's School, Repton

Christmas In The Jungle

One lonely day in the Amazon trees lay a chameleon. He thought about Christmas with all of its glee and family time around the Christmas tree. He wished for a Christmas with family and friends, wished for a Christmas where everyone came. Then, suddenly, a fairy appeared out of thin air and the warm breeze.

"Hello there, little Chameleon. I heard you wished for a Christmas tree. Luckily for you, your wish will come true!"

The fairy disappeared with a flash. In the distance, there was the sound of carols and Christmas cheer all jolly. Now the chameleon knew Christmas.

Eliz Ahmet (10)

St Wystan's School, Repton

Lightning Vs Fire

One day in Valhalla, a god called Chad woke up. Chad wasn't really a god until the day his father, Thor, gave him an element to guard with his life. It was fire.

One day, Chad heard his father laughing. Chad looked. Thor, his father, was shooting lightning bolts down to Earth, sending fires to kill people that he didn't like. Chad looked behind him and there stood Uncle Loki.

"He's up to something. You should stop him. After all, you are the god of fire."

"I will!"

He ran across the rainbow bridge to the human world to help...

Teddy Tony Myers-Saunders (8)

St Wystan's School, Repton

Dessert Island

The waves were crashing around my head. The boat capsized. I hit the rocks. I could feel blood pouring from my forehead. It felt like my life was slipping away. I knew the only way to survive was to swim for my life! I got to the beach and then I saw a sign saying *Dessert Island*. Wow, the people here really couldn't spell, could they?

I was so hungry. I decided to explore. As I got closer, I saw an array of magnificent dishes: cheesecake, trifles and ice cream plants everywhere!

"Who cares about being rescued? I'm staying forever."

Grace Amber Thompson (10)

St Wystan's School, Repton

The Two Great Rulers!

There lived a powerful god called Thor. He was the god of thunder. His dad, Odin, was the god of wisdom and poetry, and Loki was the god of mischief and mayhem.

On a dark, gloomy night, Thor the Great heard Odin and Loki squabbling fiercely over who would rule the world. He shouted, "Stop, stop! We don't need to be arguing over this".

Eventually, they decided to all be friends and rule the magnificent kingdom together.

Rather than being aggressive and selfish, you need to be kind and caring to one another to make the world a better place.

Isabel Gavin-Jones (8)
St Wystan's School, Repton

Young Samurai

It all began when a samurai master entered Earth after destroying his third planet. This samurai was called Tai Kun. Tai Kun targeted Earth's hero, Bailey. He had no superpowers and didn't wear pants over his trousers, but still stopped everything that came in his path.

Bailey casually went out for dinner at night until he saw a shadow. The shadow got closer until it stopped. Tai Kun attempted to stab Bailey, but Bailey got a hand to the handle of Tai Kun's sword and chucked it away! Bailey took one hit and Tai Kun was never seen again...

Nathan Joseph Bhardwaj (9)
St Wystan's School, Repton

Astrid The Almighty

The village got a warning from the people saying that a big troll was coming to attack them soon. Astrid was the strongest girl. Suddenly, Astrid left her hut. Everyone went silent...

Astrid set off to the forest to find the green troll. She got to the gloomy forest. Suddenly, Astrid heard a roar! She walked slowly, trying not to get caught.

She finally got to the end of the forest. Astrid could control day and night. She got her magic sword, pointed it up to the sky and it turned to day. The troll hated day! He tumbled down...

Molly Thompson (8)
St Wystan's School, Repton

The Viking Monster Mission

There was a Viking family, Astrid, Freya, Thorgrim and Taragon. They were sent on a daring mission to catch an evil monster! So, they got into their huge longship and set off. Suddenly, their boat sank and they became mermaids and mermen - but instead of finding the evil monster, they found a pot of shiny gold and money!

They swam back to the yellow, sandy shore and they sold their money and gold to help other poor people so they were not poor anymore.

But what happened to the evil, angry monster? Nobody knew about him...

Tilly Lobb (8)
St Wystan's School, Repton

The Battle Of The Gods

Thor the mighty god looks down on Earth and he sees fighting and rain making floods, sent by Loki, the mischief god. Odin was making droughts and sending sunshine.

Thor asked what they were doing. Loki said he was sending rain because the earth was parched. He asked Odin and he said he was sending heat and sunshine because there was too much water. The two gods were getting angry at each other, so they threw down more and more sun and rain in their anger.

Thor said, "Stop!"

What would happen next...?

Christopher Chenerler (7)

St Wystan's School, Repton

Revenge

Once upon a time, there lived Thor, the god of thunder. He lived in Valhalla. He was bragging that he was so amazing, fantastic and glorious.
"The gods say, 'If you're so amazing, go and catch a dragon'!"
And so he did! He climbed mountains, swam seas and walked deserts and then he finally came in sight of a dragon - but when he got closer, he finally realised that it was just a sheep dressed up as a dragon! Then, when he went back to Valhalla, he kicked everything and everyone in the city!

Malachi Xavier Easy (8)
St Wystan's School, Repton

Time Trouble

Luke found a watch and grabbed it - then, suddenly, he was in a pterodactyl nest! He escaped. He went into a portal, then a Viking was looking down on him. Suddenly, *flash!* He was running from a Roman legionnaire, charging! He was in war, a knight! He closed his eyes, hoping all of it would be over...

Suddenly, he was in the present. Luke took a sigh of relief. Suddenly, bad thumping from both sides. Vikings, Romans, knights, dinosaurs, all shouting and roaring! Luke saw the foot of a dinosaur. *Stomp!*

He woke up! He checked his wrist.

"Ohh..."

Arthur Williams (9)

Watlington Community Primary School, Watlington

Two Frenemies Meet Again

Today, Palkius was a lot more indolent than usual. He was even sleeping! Athenies managed to get him up, then Athenies became a psychic icicle! If you didn't know, Palkius had control over space. One day, 99.9% of the world was taken over by someone called Dialgus, who had control over time. Palkius and Dialgus were best, caring friends until Palkius hit Dialgus to get all the glory when saving the world together in 500AD! Dialgus stated that they would never be friends in their eternal lives. Nobody knew when this fight was going to end... It wouldn't!

Dylan Whiting (10)

Watlington Community Primary School, Watlington

The Golden Weapon

Lloyd is now travelling up the purple, colossal volcano, not knowing what dangers lie ahead. A fire dragon breathes fire at Lloyd, but Lloyd uses his powers to stop it. The dragon goes into a dive, grabbing Lloyd and putting him higher up the volcano. The energy dragon helps Lloyd and fights the fire dragon for a minute.

In the corner of his eye, Lloyd sees the golden weapon which he is searching for. Lloyd touches it and he is back home, showing his friends what it can do. He accidentally creates four dragons with elemental powers!

Ollie Saw (9)

Watlington Community Primary School, Watlington

Pigothy And The Burial Robbery

Pigothy was a unique detective because he was a pig. He liked wearing suits for work with black jeans and wore glasses.

One day, his boss called, saying that Pigothy had to go to the Anglo Saxon times and solve a crime. Pigothy grabbed a fingerprint scanner, got into a time machine and off he went. He landed next to the burial site and he looked for fingerprints. He found one! The print he found belonged to a thief. Pigothy found out where the crook lived and arrested the robber. As a reward, Pigothy claimed one million gold coins!

Alex Waterman (9)

Watlington Community Primary School, Watlington

Jay Cannon And The Pot Of Gold

My name is Jay Cannon. I live with my father Alfie Cannon. I enjoy travelling to places I never dreamed existed. I eventually find a cave that I think will lead to some underground lake - but I'm wrong. Instead, I find a pot of gold! I'm not too far from home, so I run as fast as I possibly can back to our house to tell my father of my discovery. When we get back from the cave, we find a white, mysterious letter at our front door...

Harrison Lake Cannon (10)

Watlington Community Primary School, Watlington

YOUNG WRITERS INFORMATION

We hope you have enjoyed reading this book – and that you will continue to in the coming years.

If you're a young writer who enjoys reading and creative writing, or the parent of an enthusiastic poet or story writer, do visit our website **www.youngwriters.co.uk**. Here you will find free competitions, workshops and games, as well as recommended reads, a poetry glossary and our blog. There's lots to keep budding writers motivated to write!

If you would like to order further copies of this book, or any of our other titles, then please give us a call or order via your online account.

Young Writers
Remus House
Coltsfoot Drive
Peterborough
PE2 9BF
(01733) 890066
info@youngwriters.co.uk

Join in the conversation!
Tips, news, giveaways and much more!

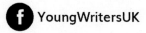 YoungWritersUK   @YoungWritersCW